"*When We Wake in Heaven* is one of the most beautiful books I have read in recent times. A book about remembering, it reminds me of the famous Buddhist statement: *Show me your original face, the face you had before your parents were born."* —Fiona Hyde

"I absolutely LOVE this book. It drew me in from the start." —Kim Smith

"Beautifully written and immensely engaging, *When We Wake In Heaven* spans continents, religions and cultures, and asks one of life's enduring questions: does the afterlife really exist and what will you find when you get there."—Muriel Cooper

"Tan Lee's book tells of humble stories of grief, loss and death, as she eloquently weaves the meaning of heaven to those on earth: it feels like a readable 'hug' and one you will want to return to." —Dr. Sue Brown

"I felt so many different emotions during the read thru. It bought me to tears, actual tears. Plus, lots of other emotions – sadness, warmth, joy, peace, hope." —Libby Holden

"Touching interweaving stories offers grace and deep comfort for anyone grappling with grief" —Jo Falvey

"I love this book!" —Christine Dvoracek

"Tan is a masterful storyteller. She has a way of unearthing worlds that feel familiar, and yet have you questioning, listening, thinking, and longing to be anchored there long enough to uncover your own deeper understanding. Her work is both economical and lyrical, heartful and humorous - a sign of a true artist." —Klaire Johnston

"*When We Wake in Heaven* is a warm-hearted tale told from several people's perspectives. We feel their pain, and delight in their joys as they travel life's journey. Tan Lee is a gifted writer who sees into the souls of her characters, bringing them to life on the page." —Kate Feher

"But you must know that i have enjoyed this tremendously and laughed to tears but also cried. This is so beautifully written." —Hélène Malavieille

Published in Australia by
TLC Publishing
PO Box 352, Mt Martha VIC 3934
www.tlcpublishing.com.au

First published in Australia 2026

National Library of Australia Cataloguing in Publication entry

A catalogue record for this book is available from the National Library of Australia

ISBN 978-1-7643931-4-0 (paperback)
ISBN 978-1-7643931-3-3 (hardcover)
ISBN 978-1-7643931-1-9 (epub)

Cover design by Blue Wren Books
Layout and design by Sophie White Design
Printed by Kindle Direct Publishing

WHEN WE WAKE IN HEAVEN

A metaphysical novel of the afterlife,
soul remembrance,
and spiritual awakening

Tan Lee

CONTENTS

This book is dedicated

to all who've lost

those they love

May you find peace

Remembering the families and friends
of Callum, Cassie and Flynn,
who passed too young

Goodbyes are only for those
who love with their eyes.
For those who love with heart
and soul, there is no separation.

— TikTok Rumi

PROLOGUE

The Hopeful Beginning

The heavens roared, a sound that rippled through the formless ether of the universe until its farthest edges quivered.

"Someone has to remind them who they are!" boomed The Source of All Things.

Older spirits turned away from this call. Their glow—steady with eons of being—dimmed at the memory of Earth. They knew the weight of human existence: how a soul could forget its purpose in that dimension, how its belief systems clung to you like mud, shrouding the light. It was easy to get lost there. To give up your mission entirely.

A squeaky voice cut through the solemn silence. "I will!"

All turned to Isaiah, a bright, newly formed being with a mischievous sparkle.

"You won't know how to deliver the message until you arrive," an ancient spirit warned, its form little more than a wisp of light.

"Or who the message is for," added another.

"Sometimes you don't even realize you're doing it," said a third.

"Sounds like a fun challenge," Isaiah replied.

A massive, swirling nebula of energy drifted

closer—one of the Oversouls, guardian of traffic to and from the earthly plane. “You understand the cost?”

“I understand the benefits,” Isaiah shot back, his light throbbing with irrepressible joy.

The elders showed no offense at this jab at their own reluctance. There was no compulsion to return to Earth. Many had already paid their dues, pushing against the darkness that waited there, again and again and again.

“So be it!” The Source declared.

With a loud pop, Isaiah vanished.

Other young souls, catching fire from his enthusiasm, spoke up.

“I haven’t been before.”

“Deal me in.”

“I’ll tag along.”

Pop! Pop! Pop! One by one, they followed Isaiah’s trail. Murmurs spread through the crowd as the others watched them go.

“I hope they do it,” said one, with a flicker of worry in its light.

“Don’t you love their enthusiasm?” said another, shimmering with fond warmth.

“The message will need to be delivered in their first years,” said an older soul, its wisdom as palpable as the pull of a black hole. “Or else they’ll forget, like everyone else.”

“The problem is,” said a soul who’d spent lifetimes on Earth, “no one listens to children.”

“No one believes those on death’s door either,”

added another voice. "Even though the dying can see us again."

"Drugs crack open the veil that blocks us out."

"Any kind of hallucination can reopen the door."

"Meditation too."

A hum spread as a message from Source pulsed through the throng.

"It's going to work. People will listen this time. They're awakening to the truth."

Hope spread like wildfire.

Beneath Its vast wings, The Source of All Things crossed Its fingers. Even It knew humans were... unpredictable.

CHAPTER ONE

The Grieving Widow

Did the Good Lord have no pity? Could He not see that her savings were drained? That she had a four-year-old to support? She was a good woman; she was. Had worked hard all her life. Said her prayers each night on stiff and swollen knees. And this was her reward? How was she supposed to take care of Isaiah with her husband gone and arthritis singing in her bones? She didn't mind for herself—living or dying felt much the same. But she wanted better for her son. A boy's shot at life shouldn't be over before he even got the chance to begin.

These thoughts gnawed at Mercy as she greeted one guest after another in the cold fellowship hall. Nearby, the radiator clanked and hissed, its weak warmth no match for the winter chill seeping through the walls. The room was small, plain, and crowded: folding chairs jammed up tight against wooden tables, mourners balancing coffee cups and paper plates of fried chicken elbow-to-elbow. Voices murmured softly, laughter layered over tears. Everyone was here to celebrate her husband's life, short as it was, but Mercy couldn't feel the joy of it, only the bleakness of the days waiting beyond the frosted windows.

The young pastor, bless him, didn't understand the depth of her struggles.

"You can rest easy," he said with a kind smile, teeth gleaming white against dark skin, like sunlight breaking through the clouds. "Your husband is free from his suffering and now lives in eternal glory with Our Lord."

"Amen," said a nearby mourner.

"I hope he's resting easy. He surely had a nasty disease," said Ebony, Mercy's younger sister, standing close on her other side. They were both in their early thirties, of medium build, with thick crowns of black braids—but years bent over washing and cleaning had curved Mercy's back and hardened her hands, while Ebony's work as an aide at Needmore kindergarten kept her skin smooth.

Pastor Thomas pressed his fingertips together. "The doctor says many of our men are struggling with that lung disease—COPD."

Mercy didn't know what COPD meant. She only understood that she'd watched her husband struggle for every breath, never knowing when the last would be. Torture for them both.

"He done told his boss a window needed to be put in that welding workshop. There was no place for the fumes to go. Nothing to sop them up but a man's lungs." No one suggested she sue. The garage had been a rinky-dink operation, since closed down and moved elsewhere. Besides, who had the money for lawyers?

"It ain't right he suffered so," said Ebony, giving Mercy's shoulders a firm, knowing squeeze.

Pastor Thomas studied the packed room. "A lot of folks sure have come to honor him."

Ebony's chin lifted. "There's family here from every corner of the state. He was a good man. No reason for him to be in the ground, unlike some."

Mercy followed her sister's gaze toward the only white person in the room. The woman loomed over the repast table, a fat Persian cat preening in her lap as she pressed tidbits into its mouth. Mercy wished she were that cat. That she had someone to pamper her like that. Her husband had been the one to keep the wolf from their door. The one who'd soothed her worries with his steady certainties. How was she going to cope all on her lonesome? Starting with the rent due next week.

"I'm gonna miss him so bad," she wailed, choking back a sob. Isaiah had clung to her side like a shadow for days, and she didn't want him to see the depths of her distress. She glanced down at her son, her hand smoothing the back of his head. "Your daddy was the sweetest soul, baby. He loved us both so much."

Ebony gave her a shrewd look, then pulled a parcel from her bag.

"Look here, Izzy, a present."

His brows drew together. "For me?"

"Uh-huh."

"It ain't my birthday."

"We're celebrating your daddy's arrival at the Pearly Gates."

Isaiah reached for the clumsily wrapped gift. "Oh,

Momma, lookee, lookee! A plane." His hands caressed the metal, as if it was made of genuine silver and not bought from the five-and-dime store.

"They're the wings carrying your daddy up to paradise," she said with a sigh, the tension in her shoulders loosening for the first time that day. Her son's fascination with this rare gift meant she wouldn't have to occupy him herself. *Bless her sister's heart!*

"Thankee, Antee." Isaiah raised his face to them and his mouth formed a small O of surprise. "Why you crying? Ain't you happy my daddy's gone to heaven?"

"So happy, Angel," said Ebony, stroking his cheek with her thumb.

"We're crying tears of joy," added Mercy, brushing the wetness from her face with the back of her hand.

There was a blur of motion, and the plane was pulled from Isaiah's grasp. An older boy raced around the room, holding it high. Pastor Thomas grabbed the young man's collar as he sailed by on his second loop of the room.

"Now, now, son, that belongs to Isaiah." He extracted the shiny object from a clenched fist.

"But I like it, sir!"

"You surely do. Maybe your momma will buy you one."

"She surely won't," spat the boy. "My momma's the meanest woman in this whole town."

"Out of the mouths of babes," muttered Ebony.

Mercy turned her head toward the figure dominating the repast table. Even from a distance, she could hear the protests as helpings for each plate were doled out, spoons and ladles kept within reach of only one pair of hands. But there was nothing she could do to help her guests. Not when the woman was the pastor's housekeeper. Here, at his request.

"She's your mother, son," said Pastor Thomas. "You need to show her respect."

The boy stuck out his tongue and ran off.

Mercy thanked the pastor for his help. It was a relief to know that the robbery had occurred within his orbit. If the plane had been pulled from her son in the yard, they might never have seen it again.

"Why don't you take your toy for a spin around the room?" Pastor Thomas suggested to Isaiah.

Her son looked at her for approval. "Momma?"

Mercy nodded, eager to be free of her maternal responsibilities. The moment he darted away, a howl of grief tore from her throat. It was a relief to finally give voice to the feelings she'd held so tightly.

Relatives, friends, and passing acquaintances filed up in slow procession to offer their condolences. Each joyful recollection about her late husband, another stab to her heart. There was sobbing, wailing and laughter. Loving memories of a life lived in service to others. And there was her sister and the pastor to lean on whenever she felt herself sinking beneath grief. As the stream petered out and more mourners headed for the repast table, Mercy thanked the pastor for hosting the homegoing.

He held up his hands in protest. "You had people

spilling out of your home into darkness at the wake. We couldn't have that after the service. Not with everyone needing supper before they headed home."

The warmth in his amber eyes overwhelmed her. "I don't know that I deserve this kindness. I ain't done nothing special."

He held her gaze. "Everybody is somebody, Mercy."

The church motto. Still, she never expected to be somebody herself. "We'll clean up the hall before we go, right?" She nudged her sister.

Ebony nodded. "We've got plenty of helping hands here."

"You don't need to worry about that," said Pastor Thomas. "Connie'll do it."

They glanced across the room at his housekeeper, locked in argument with mourners over the size of their allocated portions.

"I bet she will," murmured Ebony. Mercy shared her sister's skepticism. There was no knowing how much food would end up in her pile and how much in the housekeeper's secret stash. But before she could remind her sister of the need to be respectful to Connie Moore in the pastor's presence, her body folded in on itself.

Pastor Thomas caught her and set her back on her feet.

Ebony threw her a shrewd look. "When was the last time you ate, sis?"

She shook her head. "I dunno." It had been a trying day. She'd been too preoccupied with events to think about putting food in her mouth.

"Let's go fix you some supper. *We'll* serve ourselves."

New ladles were collected from a tiny kitchen adjacent to the hall, and two plates piled high. She managed to swallow a few bites of fried chicken and collard greens before Connie Moore descended on her.

"How you plan on managing, Mercy, without your husband to pay the bills?"

For such a tiny woman, her voice sure carried. Heads swiveled toward the demure brown-haired middle-aged figure whose soft appearance hid a backbone of steel.

Mercy felt a protective arm wrap around her shoulders. "Don't you go worrying about that!" Ebony had raised her voice to meet Connie's sharp tone. "Black folks look after their own. Anyways, I thought you were too busy guarding that tomato aspic as if it was gold, to have time for a word to us."

Connie licked her fingers. "I ate the last piece."

"You finished the great hunk that was left on that plate?"

One eyebrow lifted. "I wouldn't call it a hunk."

"I surely would." Ebony's eyes darted fire.

Mercy winced, wishing her sister wouldn't bait the woman so. Thankfully, her snide comments were ignored.

A flicker of weariness crossed Connie's face quickly masked. "Y'all know the cook?"

"You're looking at her," said Ebony.

Mercy felt a poke in her ribs and found her voice. "Glad you liked it, Mrs. Moore."

"You must give me the recipe." It was a command rather than a request.

She bowed her head. "Yes, ma'am."

Isaiah zoomed past them, plane high in the air, and Connie nodded at him. "You should control that child, Mercy. He's causing a rumpus."

"There's only one child causing—"

Mercy put a warning hand on her sister's arm. "You're right, Mrs. Moore. He should be eating his supper with the rest of us." She called out to Isaiah's retreating back, "You hungry, baby?"

"Yes-ee!" he replied, tucking the plane under his arm as he hurried over. "I spy with my little eye..." He scanned the repast table right to the end. "Sweet potato pie."

Her chest clenched. That had been her husband's favorite.

Connie leaned across the table to poke Isaiah. "You the man of the house now. Gonna step up, boy?"

Arms whipped Isaiah away. "Let's go getcha pie, Izzy. Coming, Mercy?"

Ebony was already striding off with him, so Mercy hurried after them with her plate. Her sister cut an enormous slice for Isaiah, and they settled in a far corner, away from Connie's sharp eyes.

"What's a house man, Antee?" asked Isaiah, poking his fork into the pie's golden filling.

"Don't you fret about it, Izzy. That woman only

wants to scare you some. She loves seeing other folks' trouble too much."

Mercy combed her son's hair with her fingers as he ate on her lap, finding comfort in the simple gesture. "You enjoying your supper, baby?"

"Yes, Momma, but"—Isaiah gulped down the last bite—"I gotta get Daddy to heaven." He hopped down onto the wooden floorboards, propelling his plane upward again as if it was the actual vehicle transporting his father to the afterlife.

Pastor Thomas reappeared as Mercy pushed away her half-empty plate. "Connie'll wrap up the leftovers for you to take home." He looked across at his housekeeper, who was clearing tables nearby. "Won't you?"

She glared at him.

"I'll give you a hand, Mrs. Moore." Ebony winked at Mercy, who smiled back with gratitude. One of them needed to keep an eye on how the remnants were divvied up. She wondered for the umpteenth time why the pastor had taken Connie Moore in.

Grief made people do strange things. There were whispers of a beloved wife who'd died in childbirth and a baby stillborn. That he'd moved to their church to escape these memories, and refused to consider marrying again. There was comfort in knowing she wasn't alone in mourning a partner who couldn't be replaced, but why had he chosen a mean-spirited white woman as his companion instead?

The sky darkened and mourners began to take

their leave. She kept them talking as long as possible, reluctant to let anyone go. Each departure felt like a dimming of her husband's presence. Gone was the boy who'd asked for her hand as a teenager. The man who insisted on walking curbside when they ventured into town. Who hadn't pressed her when pregnancy was slow to bloom in her body, and who'd never failed to kiss her first thing in the morning and last thing at night. How did you let go of a good 'un? The thought buckled her and a fresh wave of grief swept her under.

A man in his forties with a neatly trimmed head of black curls came up to say goodbye. "Is there anything I can do for you, Mercy?"

She gathered herself. "No thanks, doctor. I appreciate you coming and all the help you gave my husband."

He turned his hands upward. "I wish there was more I could have done."

"The drugs you provided eased his pain," she reassured him.

He ran a hand over his mouth. "That's something I guess. How's your arthritis?"

"Same ol' same ol'."

"Let me know if it gets worse and I'll give you something for it."

She nodded, but, truth be told, she couldn't afford to fill prescriptions, not even at the rundown drugstore that served her community on the outskirts of town.

Three sets of arms appeared before them with loaded boxes.

"Lordy!" Her vision blurred anew at this kindness. At least there'd be food on the table for the next week.

The pastor and Ebony talked softly of how her husband would rejoice to see her cared for, while Connie stood to one side, throwing daggers at them with her eyes. A tug at her dress begged for her attention, but she swatted the small hand away. She couldn't deal with that hand. Not now. She had years stretching in front of her to answer that call, but only moments left to say goodbye to the man she'd lain with in a contented marriage bed. She wanted to drown herself in thoughts of him while she still could.

Isaiah's reedy voice rose into the conversation. "Are you crying tears of joy again, Momma?"

Her mouth tightened as she looked down at him. "No, baby, I'm feeling low 'cause your daddy's gone to heaven."

He blinked. "You don't need to be sad, Momma. When we wake in heaven, we's happy."

She startled. He sounded so sure of himself. "I hope so, baby. I truly hope so."

"We is," Isaiah insisted. "I seen heaven with my own eyes."

Heads turned. Even the doctor lingered.

"You've seen heaven? When?" she asked.

"Before here."

"You remember the before?"

His little eyebrows knit together. "Don't you, Momma?"

"No, baby. What's it like?"

"It's a big, sunny garden where everyone's smiling. There's the greenest grass you ever saw and fields and fields of flowers. People sing and dance all day long, even the animals and trees join in." His eyes shone as he spoke, as if he saw this glorious vision before him.

"Sounds like Narnia," murmured Ebony. Mercy knew her sister had been reading him that children's tale while she tended to her dying husband.

Isaiah nodded vigorously. "But the Ice Queen is good, and there's no sun or moon, only lots and lots of light. That's God's love shining on us. We sparkle in heaven, like we's diamonds."

"Sounds mighty fine," said the doctor, patting him on the shoulder. "Hope I get there."

"Everyone gets there," said Isaiah.

"Are you sure about that?" asked Ebony. Mercy's mouth twitched at the side-eye her sister was giving the housekeeper.

"Yup!"

"Well, I'll be," said Connie, staring at him with a strange look on her face.

Pastor Thomas pursed his lips. "That's a delightful story, son, but not everyone makes it to heaven. We have to go through judgment first."

Isaiah's forehead wrinkled.

"Hush now, baby," said Mercy, not wanting her boy to upset the reverend. Not after his kindness. "He knows the Good Book better than we do."

The crease on Isaiah's forehead deepened, but thank the Lord, he held his tongue, just like she'd taught him.

The pastor touched the plane in Isaiah's hands. "Has your daddy reached heaven yet?"

Isaiah raised his toy aloft. "I's taking him there." He zoomed off, wings slicing the air.

Pastor Thomas turned to Mercy. "Your son's got a mighty fine imagination."

"He's a believer, that's all," she said.

"Does he know about the Old Testament prophet he's named after? Maybe he's taken that story to heart."

"Only what he hears in church."

"Isaiah a family name?"

She shook her head in wonder at what she was about to confess. "He was gonna be John, after my daddy—another good man, may he rest in peace—but the moment I held him in my arms, Isaiah popped into my head, as if he was telling me what to call him."

The doctor massaged his chin. "If your son's paying attention in church, he deserves a proper education."

She wasn't sure what he meant by that. No one in her family had stayed in school long, but they'd learned the basics. Their teachers had made sure of it.

"We've got the best black educators in the state in Starkville," the doctor continued, pressing his point.

"Ain't that the truth! I only wish Isaiah wouldn't take sermons so literally. Better have a word with him," said Pastor Thomas, heading outside toward where the plane had flown. The doctor followed him a moment later.

A box was thrust at Mercy. "See you Tuesday," said

Connie. The doctor followed him a moment later.

"Yes, ma'am."

"What's on Tuesday?" asked Ebony after the housekeeper sauntered off, the cat slinking in her wake, its tail held high.

She sighed. "Rent day." Connie Moore was not only the pastor's housekeeper, but a local landlord. Her landlord.

The muscles in Ebony's jawline tensed. "Has that woman no shame? Talking about money when your husband's still warm in his grave. I'm gonna give her a piece of my mind."

She held her sister back. "Leave it! I need her on my side."

Her sister scowled. "What's a white woman doing owning Black folks' homes anyways? Why doesn't she work at her brother's drugstore instead of sticking her nose in our business?"

The question was so ridiculous that Mercy smiled. "Most things are owned by white people. And her brother runs a tight ship. I reckon he'd give her a world of trouble."

Ebony laughed. "Ain't that the truth."

They both understood the social hierarchy in their town. A white woman could get away with speaking sharply to Black folks but was subject to her own restrictions.

Mercy sighed. "Lord, how am I going to make ends meet with the little bit of cleaning and washing work I get in town?"

"We'll find a way," said Ebony.

Her mouth pulled into a brittle smile. "You're as poor as I am."

"God'll provide."

Would He? Her heart sagged under the weight of doubt. The rent due, the empty bed, the ache in her bones—none of it felt touched by heaven. She felt smaller than ever, a woman left to weather a storm alone.

Then Isaiah swooped back into her arms, his small body warm against hers. She gazed down at him, his face alight with the certainty of children. *A sunny garden. Diamonds in the light.* The words shimmered in her mind, fragile but insistent. Maybe it was a sign. A reminder that the Lord still walked beside her, unseen but ready to answer her prayers. She gathered her son close, pressing her cheek into his curls. Maybe, just maybe, she hadn't been abandoned after all.

CHAPTER TWO

The Cynical Doctor

It was only a block from the subway to Ethan's workplace, but he kept his head low, not wanting any trouble. In the washed-out morning light, the hospital loomed ahead; the letters of its name weeping down the back wall. From the parking lot came a blare of horns, sharp and impatient.

"Help me!"

"Help me!"

"Help me!"

Inside, the emergency room was as busy as ever. Bodies crammed into hard plastic seats, each with its own story of broken bones and hidden tumors, cancer or heart disease. An old woman held her stomach, while a baby leaked green snot down its mother's arms, and a cloth pressed against a young man's side slowly turned red. Pain hung in the air, yet an eerie silence filled the space. In the short time Ethan had worked here, he'd learned that only people with privilege complained. Those with little were just grateful someone cared.

A loud moan—the sound heavy and jarring in the quiet—broke the tension.

He grabbed a young woman as she collapsed before him, easing her down onto a cushioned bench with a circular pattern that was enough to give anyone head spins. Nurses and medics poured out of doors.

"Good catch," said someone.

An intern threw him a quizzical look. "Started your shift early?"

"Apparently," he replied with a smile.

"We've got this," said Dinah, a senior nurse. "You wouldn't want blood or vomit on that nice jacket of yours."

He handed the unconscious woman over and headed for the locker room, inspecting his clothes as he wove through the corridors. She was right. He didn't want to damage his new winter coat. Fox fur didn't come cheap. There'd be no similar purchases in his immediate future, not on a resident's salary.

A brief meeting took place at the change of shift, and he was sent on his way with a stack of printouts. There was an old man short of breath, getting no relief from the nebulizer. A twenty-five-year-old woman complaining of severe pain in her lower right side. Definitely appendicitis. Stapling of knife wounds after a robbery. A baby wheezing with RSV—a nasty virus in infants under six months, though this one looked stable. An elderly victim of a hit-and-run. All told, a delicious smorgasbord of trauma to dig into.

That's why he'd chosen Lincoln, despite his boyfriend's misgivings about the area's high crime rate. He was on a mission to become one of the best emergency doctors in the country without leaving his native city. The cases here, raw and relentless, provided the exact crucible needed to forge his skills. His Spanish was improving too, an advantage when applying for a permanent position on the Upper East Side, home to the city's most prestigious hospitals. It was only logical they'd want him after he proved himself in the hardest training ground in the city.

"Finished already?" asked Dinah when he returned to the desk for more cases. He couldn't tell if the sour expression on her face was due to disapproval or the tightly coiled bun at the back of her head.

"That's how I roll," he replied, with a grin.

Dinah didn't smile, even though she'd been cackling with the other nurses moments before. She just handed over more printouts and sent him on his way. He ignored the snub. What mattered was forming a diagnosis and plan of care in record time to free up beds and, more importantly, impress the senior residents, whose opinions were the only ones that truly counted.

But there were interruptions to the smooth flow of his morning.

An old woman's bags sprawled across the floor, forming a barrier in his path. At the top of the pile, a white plastic bag bobbed up and down of its own volition. Homeless patients often smuggled pets into the ER. There'd even been whispers of a snake slithering down a corridor recently. He high-stepped through the makeshift obstacle course, reluctant to discover this one's secret.

A throng gathered around a gurney, and he shoved

to the front of the pack, where a gunshot victim lay swaddled in wires and bedding like a mummy.

"He hasn't leveled out," said the surgeon in charge. "Let's get him up to ICU."

Ethan was only too happy to assist his superior. Dinah intercepted him on the way back and handed over another chart.

"Thirty-nine-year-old woman with high blood pressure."

"I was going to—"

She cut him off. "You should see this one first."

The case didn't sound pressing, not when a head wound awaited, but he marched into a nearby bay, skimming the paperwork.

"So...you have a history of high blood pressure. Are you taking medication for that?"

"I, er, used to."

He looked up. A large African American woman shifted in her chair, her shirt straining at the seams. "Not anymore?"

"I been busy lately."

He frowned. "Too busy to take your meds? Sounds like you need to slow down."

She leaned back, exhaling with a groan. "How'm I 'sposed to do that when I'm workin' three jobs."

"Are you working those jobs to make rent?"

"Mm-hmm."

He crossed his arms. "Here's the deal. Your blood pressure's out of control, and you smoke, right? Both these things will turn your kidneys to mush, then you'll end up on dialysis and won't be able to work at all. But you can turn things around right now by taking your meds."

"Okay, sure doctor, I will."

He could tell from the blankness in her eyes that she wasn't listening. She'd be back, squandering their time before the month was out. What was wrong with people? Why ignore facts? They were fortunate to live in an age where science held all the answers. Yet some deliberately chose to remain in the dark ages, clinging to ignorance and wishful thinking.

"That was quick," said Dinah, as Ethan pushed back through the curtains, another hideous choice of fabric, but with rectangles instead of circles.

He shrugged. "The woman has a diagnosis but won't take her meds. What can I do?"

"Keep her—"

He held out his hand. "What's next?" He'd sew up the knife wound waiting in the next bay and tear through whatever else she handed him. Anything to shut her up.

She slapped more paperwork into his open palm.

A scuffle broke out in the hallway beside them.

"I'm not staying here. Get off me, you queers!" Two NYPD officers shoved a boy—who couldn't have been older than ten—back into his seat. Ethan winced and moved on.

The laceration was stitched. A broken ankle revealed hidden high blood pressure. The baby with green snot had a bacterial infection that required antibiotics. A superficial graze across the shoulder needed cleaning and dressing.

"Is my time up?" asked the elderly man, who'd shot himself in the leg while cleaning his gun.

"Not today," said Ethan, closing the shallow wound with quick, practiced stitches.

The man's wrinkled face creased into a smile. There were more gaps inside his mouth than teeth. "Wouldn't matter. I've lived a good life. Never shot anyone, except myself. God'll let me through those pearly gates."

"Is that right?" Ethan placed a dressing over the stitches. "There you go. Keep the bandage clean and dry. Take the antibiotics as directed. And pay more attention next time you're cleaning that gun."

The man grasped his hand. "God will reward you for this goodness."

Ethan shrugged off the benediction as he headed back to the nurse's station. God hadn't been there during his parents' divorce. Not when his father deserted the family for a pretty young thing at his brokerage firm. And certainly not when his mother retreated to bed, leaving him to fend for himself in the wreckage. He'd barely been fourteen. How could parents abandon their only child like that? At least medicine was logical. Science was *his* god.

Dinah made no comment about his speed as she handed over another chart. "End of the corridor. Woman with a sore back."

"That's it?" he grumbled, seeing only a single

paragraph in the notes.

"Uh-huh." Her eyes had already returned to the computer screen in front of her.

He raised his voice. "Why isn't she seeing her primary care? Or a chiropractor? What's she doing here clogging up the ER?"

The fury in her return whisper was unmistakable. "Keep your voice down. You know as well as I do, it's cheaper to come to us."

His jaw clenched. This wasn't the type of case he'd signed up for, but what could he do? It was his first month on the job, too early to make waves.

Inside the bay, a middle-aged Latina woman sat panting on the gurney.

"Sorry...feel like I've run a mile. I was finishing paperwork...in the office...few blocks away."

Her words washed over him as he pulled on gloves, eager to get the consult over with. "Where do you hurt?"

She pointed to her upper back.

He pressed on the area, and she flinched. "How long's it been sore?"

"Since...yesterday."

"And on a scale of 1-10, how would you rate it?"

"Started at two...Now...eight?"

He laid a hand on her forehead: clammy. Pulled a stethoscope from his coat.

"I haven't been myself...for a while. Nauseous... dizzy. This pain's...off...on."

He listened to the murmurs of her heart. There was

some message it was trying to tell him. "When did the symptoms start?"

"Few weeks...ago."

He lifted his head. "And you haven't been to see a doctor?"

"Yes...He said stress...Who doesn't?...But back pain... intense...Didn't think...could wait." Suddenly, her face drained of color and she collapsed to the floor.

"What the hell?" He took her pulse, slammed the emergency button, and started compressions.

Medical staff burst into the bay, hands sliding beneath her body.

"On my count," said Dinah. "One, two, three..."

He stopped pumping while others lifted his patient onto the gurney.

"What's the story?" asked an intern, taking over the compressions.

"I..." He wasn't sure.

The hot, metallic tang of adrenaline hung in the air, mingling with the sterile bite of latex and alcohol wipes—a cocktail of panic and purpose that clung to every breath.

"She's having a heart attack," said Dinah.

"There's no chest pain!" he protested.

"Symptoms are different in women." Her words landed sharp as a slap across the face, and he felt their implication. *He should have known that if he was on the fast track.*

"Let's shock," he said.

The patient's shirt was pulled open, and someone

attached pads to her chest.

"Charging," said a doctor. "Clear?"

"Clear," murmured a few voices.

A button was pressed. "Shock delivered."

Dinah's hands wrapped around the woman's wrist. "No pulse yet."

"One, two, three, four...," said the intern, pushing on the patient's chest. Another medic placed a mask over the patient's mouth and breathed into it.

"Again!" said Ethan.

"Clear?"

"Clear!"

"Nothing," said Dinah, her hands on the wrist again.

He ran a hand through his hair. "No pulse?"

Dinah raised her eyebrows. She clearly thought he was an idiot.

"Again," he said.

"Clear!"

"Shock delivered."

"Slight pulse," said Dinah. "Very weak." She attached an oximeter to the patient's finger.

His eyes flicked to the monitor. The woman's oxygen levels were dangerously low. "Get a high-flow oxygen mask on her. Now!"

A different device was secured over her nose and mouth, its reservoir bag inflating as oxygen rushed in. Her chest rose and fell more steadily, a hint of color returning to her cheeks. Calm settled over the room. Everyone filed out except for two.

"Can you start IV heparin, bolus, then infusion?"

he asked Dinah. It was standard protocol after a suspected heart attack to prevent clotting.

For once, there were no snide looks. She hurried off to do his bidding.

The patient stirred.

"Hello there," he said, gazing down at her. "You gave us quite the scare." She clawed at the prongs up her nose, and he lifted them away. "You're breathing on your own. That's a good sign. Do you know where you are?" He checked her eyes for orientation.

She nodded weakly. "Hospital...ER."

"Good," he said, relief softening his tone. "How are you feeling?"

She scanned the room as if the answer might be written on the walls. Finally, her eyes found his. "My heart stopped, didn't it?"

"What? Yes!" *Lucky guess on her part.*

"I saw you working on me."

"You were out the entire time," he scoffed.

Her gaze remained fixed on him. "I know this sounds crazy, but I floated out of my body while you were trying to restart my heart. Ended up on that ceiling looking down."

They both glanced upward, as if expecting to see her spirit still lingering there.

She turned back to him. "That's how I know I had a heart attack."

He shook his head. *Impossible.* She'd been clinically dead.

"I saw myself on the floor. You hit a button, and

people rushed into the room. Everyone was in a frenzy."

He crossed his arms. *So far. So standard. She could've picked that up from any medical drama on TV.*

"You said, 'What the hell!'" she added.

"I beg your pardon."

"Before you hit the button, you said, 'What the hell!'"

Another lucky guess.

"You shocked me back on the third go, and I still had a weak pulse. It was the nurse who knew I was having a heart attack, wasn't it?"

"Well, yeees—"

"You weren't expecting it."

"I guess I wasn't, but—"

"But you saved my life," finished the woman. "Thank you."

Dinah returned with the heparin infusion setup and connected it to the patient's IV line.

"Anything else?" she asked.

He kept his eyes fixed on the woman on the gurney. "I'll be out in a moment with further instructions."

"O-kay..." Dinah hesitated, then stepped out.

He exhaled, considered the situation. As a scientist, he knew that consciousness was an act of physical brain function. That there was no logical way she could have been aware of what was happening after she flatlined. Yet how could he explain the things she'd seen and heard? It was medically inexplicable.

"What was it like?" he asked.

"What?"

"Being dead."

She considered a moment. "I sensed nothing. No pain, no pressure. Not even when five people had their hands all over my chest. Not something I'd usually allow." She gave a weak smile, but the joke fell flat. He was too busy mentally counting how many had been around the bed. *One, two, three, four... yep, five.*

She gazed upward again. "I could've stayed floating on that ceiling forever. It felt so peaceful up there... disconnected from the worries of the world. But the moment you jump-started my heart... I slammed back into my body...then the pain came back."

He laid a hand on her arm. "Don't talk if it's tiring." He didn't want to lose her again. What would Dinah say?

"I *want* to tell you what happened...you're my witness."

"Did you see or hear anything," he gulped, "unusual?"

A smile. "You mean supernatural? No...I guess I was in escrow."

"In what row?" *Had she hit her head in the fall?*

"Escrow. It's a type of holding account...you know, where assets are held until conditions are met...I guess I haven't fulfilled my obligations on Earth yet...My children'll be relieved about that."

"So, you floated out of your body and came back again. No God?"

"I felt warmth, like the sun was shining on my

back...Are you a believer?"

He chewed his lip. A patient had flipped out the other day when he refused to join her in prayer. He didn't want to upset this one, not in her delicate state. "A believer in which faith? Christian? Muslim? Buddhist?"

She laughed. "Take your pick. I don't think God's fussy."

"God wasn't there for my mother when my parents divorced," he said. "She prayed to Him every day for deliverance, and it never came. My father really screwed her over. We had to move downtown." He didn't bother mentioning the church's take on homosexuality. No God's love there either.

The woman cocked her head. "Maybe deliverance wasn't meant to come that way for your mama."

"She had to get a job for the first time in her life and ended up teaching troubled teens," he snapped.

"You don't approve?"

"It wasn't the life she was used to." It hadn't been the life he was accustomed to either: a cheap walk-up on the wrong side of town, evenings spent alone while his mother planned lessons and corrected assignments. His salvation hadn't come from God but from a hard-earned scholarship into med school, a life raft away from his family's sinking ship.

Her eyes fixed on his, unwavering. "How does your mama feel about her job?"

He blinked. That wasn't something he'd ever considered. An image rose of her smiling over her students' work. Laughing at their adolescent mistakes. "I think she might actually enjoy it."

"There you go then."

He bristled. "My mother didn't want to work."

"But maybe she was meant to," the woman gently replied.

"I...yes, but..."

She smiled at him. "We don't know God's plans. We just have to follow the path laid out for us."

He tugged at his collar. "Well, God's plan for you right now is an EKG and a chest X-ray. The nurse will also take some blood. Let's find out what's going on inside that chest of yours." He poked his head through the curtains and called for Dinah.

Every test came back negative.

"It doesn't make sense," he said, shaking his head over the scans hours later. "Your heart's a normal size. There's no sign of blocked arteries or issues with electrical signals. Cholesterol's within the expected range. You appear perfectly healthy."

"My back pain's gone too," said the woman, sitting up. "And I'm not breathless anymore. Maybe I'm healed?"

"Impossible!"

She winked at him. "Miracles do happen, doctor. I guess I've done whatever it was I was meant to do here."

He frowned. *What did she mean by that?*

She jumped down onto the floor. "Can I go home?"

"I, er..."

The hospital bracelet was ripped off. Clothes pulled back on. Nothing could convince her to stay. And before he could drag any other staff into the argument, she was gone.

He kept an eye out for her return—they'd never resolved the source of her pain—and even roped Dinah into watching for her on his days off. The woman never came back.

Her presence, however, lingered. The unsettling sense that the world was stranger than everything he'd learned to trust stayed with him, changing everything: how he spoke to patients, how he processed what happened to them, how he listened to the nurses.

As time went on, he found himself drawn to other patients who had *died* and returned, digging into near-death experiences online, and sketching new plans for his future—much to his boyfriend's amusement and father's horror. That single encounter altered the entire course of his life, reshaping who he wanted to be and how he would chase the impossible. Never in his wildest dreams could he have imagined where it would take him.

CHAPTER THREE

The Hopeless Hippie

The apartment door cracked open and a few disheveled heads appeared in the gap—young men in the last gasp of adolescence, a late night written across their faces.

Doh flashed his most heartwarming smile, as he always did for customers.

"Holy shit!" blurted one of the boys crowding the doorway.

"I'm blinded by the light," another drawled, pulling a pair of sunglasses down from his head to cover his eyes.

"Now I've seen it all," added a third. "Shouldn't you be into K-Pop?"

Doh ignored the jabs, handing over two plastic bags. "Three deluxe sandwiches, two waffle potato fries, nuggets, mac and cheese, six fudge brownies, two root beers, and a Sprite." He lingered on the doorstep.

"Is that everything?" asked the first, his hand hovering, ready to shut the door.

"He's looking for a tip, dude," said the second, laughter glinting in his eyes.

"I'll give you a tip," the first said with a smirk. "Tone down the tie-dye."

"No one's worn a scarf wrapped around their head since the '60s," the second chimed in.

"And you need a haircut," added the third.

The door slammed shut.

Doh's smile dissolved. He sighed and hopped back on his bicycle. Frat guys were the absolute worst. What was so wrong with a guy having long hair?

Back at the store, his boss pounced like a yappy terrier.

"These bags are cold. I keep telling you to get a moped. You're never going to make us any money on that old thing." She jabbed a finger at the rusty contraption lying on the concrete outside.

He let the lecture wash over him as he collected the new orders—if he wanted to be judged for his lifestyle choices, he'd visit his parents—and headed back out.

"First guy who shows up with a moped is taking your job!" she shouted after him.

He flashed a peace sign over his shoulder, though from behind it probably didn't look that peaceful. There was certainly no peace for him that shift as orders piled up. He worked late into the evening to keep up with demand.

K-Town was bursting into life as he biked back through its dim streets. More Latino than Asian these days, the area still felt like his home. After his parents kicked him out, he'd shacked up with a cousin in a rundown share house—a rare bargain in a neighborhood that was rapidly gentrifying. Shin was the one who'd turned him onto the '60s revolution.

Most of their downtime was spent smoking weed and listening to Bob Dylan, soaking up the mellow, hippie vibe.

"I'm back," he yelled, kicking off his shoes at the front door.

Shin appeared, another Korean American in his early twenties, although he'd actually been born here. "Got the dough?"

He held up a fistful of crumpled bills, and Shin snatched them out of his hand.

"Ed's waiting for us."

Doh gazed longingly at the couch. He'd prefer to spend the rest of the evening watching a brain-dead show on TV. Zombies shuffling through the end of the world flashed into mind. Why did people always want him to do things? His parents insisted he go to college. His boss hounded him to deliver faster. Even Shin demanded something from him. Why couldn't he just share his good vibes? Why wasn't that enough for anyone?

"We need to go," Shin pressed, steering him back out the door.

They rode to a nearby address, Shin perched precariously on the handlebars of Doh's bike. In the shadows of an apartment building, a familiar figure paced, cigarette burning between his fingers. As soon as Ed spotted them, he flicked the butt into a gutter.

"Hurry up," he snapped. "It's almost midnight. I gotta get to the clubs soon." A hefty bulldog of a man, muscles carved from hours at the gym, he was not one to argue with.

"Cool, man," said Shin. "Give us the fent and we'll be outta here."

"Hold your horses! I wanna see if this stuff sings. It's fresh off the boat from a new supplier down south."

The chunky chains on Ed's chest jangled as he led them toward a ground-floor condo. Someone else lurked in the front garden waiting for the hit: a wiry kid wearing a backwards Dodgers snapback, his jittery movements betraying the "chill" he tried to project.

"Who are you?" Shin demanded, pointing at the boy's skinny chest.

"Andres," he shot back, meeting Shin's stare head-on.

"How old are you?"

Andres stretched up on his toes. "Old enough."

Shin shot Ed a questioning look, and got a shrug in reply. Doh knew their dealer only cared about money—he'd let anyone tag along for the ride. It didn't sit right, but Ed wasn't someone you second-guessed. He kept his mouth shut, as did his cousin.

"Let's get on with it," said Andres. "We've been waiting for ages."

"He's a virgin," Ed mouthed behind the boy's back, as they moved inside.

"Nice digs," said Doh, spun out by the marble countertops and shiny steel surfaces in the kitchen, another vector in the capitalist-consumer matrix. Ed had a contact in the local real estate business, and the dude had really come through tonight. Compared with their usual drug dens, the place was palatial.

"Don't make a mess," Ed warned. "This apartment's up for sale."

He placed a glass pipe on the coffee table in the living room, and the group seated themselves in a circle around it.

Shin cocked an eyebrow. "What's the deal?"

"Latest thing from Mexico," said Ed. "Thought you'd like to try it. I know how keen you are on spiritual adventure."

Doh caught the sarcasm and stifled a smile. He didn't care about spiritual adventure either. All he wanted was to spin out and feel at peace.

Ed held out his hand. It was payment upfront. Doh winced as Shin handed over all his precious bills. He'd sweated for that sum. Spiritual adventure sure came at a steep price.

"Who's first?" Ed asked, tipping white powder into a pipe.

"Me," said Andres, leaning forward.

"Okay, kid." A strange mixture of curiosity and resignation played on Ed's face, but Doh was too tired to work out what it meant. Their dealer kept his cards close to his chest at the most open of times. Best not to know what he was thinking, really, considering the world he operated in.

Quiet draped the room as the pipe passed from hand to hand—a sacred ritual that reminded Doh of the Buddhist temple he'd visited with Shin. Only Ed abstained. He never mixed business with pleasure.

When his turn arrived, Doh drank in the smoke, letting it blur the edges of his thoughts. His parents' disappointment, their dreams of him as a doctor or lawyer, slipped away. As it should. He didn't have it in him for that kind of life. All he wanted was to smile and make people happy.

"Whoa!" Shin gasped, eyes wide. "This shit's the bomb."

Ed's gaze sharpened. "Good to hear."

"I'm feeling it too," murmured Doh, sinking back against a nearby chair.

"Oi!" Ed barked. "Don't get too comfortable. The furniture's rented."

Doh snapped back upright. "Cool, man."

Andres took another lungful, followed by Doh, who'd lost track of his place in the rotation. No one said anything when he followed it up with another hit. Shin had zoomed in on Andres.

"Sooooo, what's your deal? Are you, like, in middle school?"

"Yeah! So what?" the boy snarled.

"You're not old enough for this kind of hit."

Andres puffed out his chest. "Getting high's how boys become men." His voice faded into uncertainty on the last few words. The drug was kicking in.

Doh let out a quiet, wry breath. *Of course he thinks this makes him a man.* "Is this your first hit?" His words fell slowly, almost dreamlike.

A nod.

"Hell of an initiation you've chosen," muttered

Shin, passing the pipe back to Doh.

"I told him to start lighter," said Ed, picking at a loose fingernail. "But the kid insisted."

Doh watched the boy's tongue split into forks, the hissing growing louder, filling the room—or was that just his mind unraveling? His tongue split into forks and the hissing grew louder, enveloping the room—or was that just Doh's mind unraveling?

"What's *your* deal?" Andres shot at Shin. "Why are you here if you have such high moral standards?"

"I'm looking for answers to the big questions in life." Shin's eyes burned with fervor. Or maybe it was just the artificial juice pumping through his veins.

"Like...what?" asked Andres, his words slowing as well.

Every comment—even Ed's unspoken ones—hit Doh loud and clear. *What a bunch of losers! No one's gonna care if this goes south.*

What did their dealer mean by that? Doh's foggy mind couldn't figure it out.

Shin stared into space. "Like...why are we here? Who are we? Everyone knows drugs are the gateway to enlightenment. I'm searching for nirvana."

Andres snorted, then pointed at Doh. "What about you?"

Doh exhaled and sank back into the chair. In the hazy atmosphere, Ed didn't seem to notice this transgression. "My dream? One more day at Disneyland."

"How many times you been?"

"Once." Doh shrank further as everyone's eyes

swiveled toward him.

"Once? And you call yourself an American!" Ed was always making digs at Doh's immigration status, even though he was only second generation himself.

Doh sighed. "My parents refused to take me, except when an important auntie was visiting from Korea. And even then, I wasn't allowed to go on any of the rides because she was scared of the machinery. I'm determined to save enough tips to go back. Disneyland's *my* nirvana."

"Mine is to live at the beach," said Ed, flicking his freed fingernail across the room. Apparently, it didn't matter if *he* spoiled the furnishings. "I grew up in the Valley. Can't ever get enough of watching the waves roll in from my digs right on the Speedway in Venice."

Shin's arms stretched out. "Watch me! I'm flying."

"How can I do that?" asked Andres, sounding too far gone to be miffed.

A hush descended.

Doh's breathing slowed and slowed, until it stopped altogether. The room dissolved around him, swallowed by a pitch-black void. He floated in this moonless night for what felt like forever. There was no up, no down, no left or right—only the emptiness of space pressing in, an infinite, aching loneliness.

Low whirring broke the silence, mechanical and steady. Somewhere, a projector rolled, playing a movie in which Doh was the star. He watched his life unfold, sensing not only his own emotions but the raw, unfiltered feelings of everyone around him. An excruciating experience. His boss's frustration at

Chick-fil-A mingled with her compassion. She saw him as someone whose future was already written, and not in a good way. More unsettling was his parents' quiet grief when he walked out after their ultimatum: either college or go. A wave of guilt and shame swelled through him. He tried to turn away, but the screen followed his gaze, relentless. There was no escaping this torture.

Then, a strange thing happened. Love welled up inside, sudden and strong. For himself. The deeper he sank into his screwups, the stronger it grew, flowing through him without end. He wasn't pathetic. He wasn't worthless. For the first time, he understood that, like everyone else, he deserved some good in his life.

Darkness again. A light glowed in the distance. Within it, a figure took form—his auntie riding a carriage down a mountain, a familiar waterfall spilling silver behind her.

"Whoo-hoo!" she yelled, lifting her hands from the bars to wave at him.

His body shook and shook and shook. Voices crashed through the vision, harsh and urgent.

"Is he dead?" Andres screamed.

"Poke him!" Ed commanded.

"I'm not touching him!"

Still, the image of his auntie lingered. Somehow, Doh knew he'd join her on that ride one day.

A hand pressed his leg, pulling him back.

"He's warm," whispered Shin, voice trembling.

A sharp slap cracked across Doh's face. His eyes blinked open to see a hefty shape looming over him.

"Looks like he's back," said Ed.

Shin crouched beside him, face pale with worry. "Are you with us?"

The fuzz on his tongue loosened. "Yeah?"

"What just happened?" Andres asked, rocking back and forth in a far corner.

"I don't know, but I'm getting out of here." Ed was already stuffing the gear into his backpack.

"Don't leave this world a sinner, man," Doh croaked, feeling the need to share the flood of love that still throbbed through him.

Ed's eyes flicked up, startled. "What the hell?"

"We need to help Doh," said Shin. "He's had a seizure."

"Leave him."

Shin pulled a phone from his back pocket. "I'm calling 911."

"Your funeral," said Ed.

Doh's lips twitched. *No, it was almost my funeral.*

"You know the police'll come," Ed continued. "Don't you dare say I was here. You narc on me, you pay!"

"Is that all you can think about? Yourself? He's our friend."

"I don't have friends, I have clients."

Andres stopped rocking. "I thought you were *my* friend."

Doh pushed himself upright. "I'm...okay."

"There you go," said Ed, hoisting the backpack onto his shoulders and heading for the door.

Shin frowned. "Are you sure?"

Andres edged closer, straining to hear the answer.

Doh nodded. "Yeah...but I need to tell you something."

He felt unexpectedly clear. Every failure, every choice—it all led here, to this moment. His tone must have conveyed that certainty because even Ed stayed to listen. He reached for words, trying to explain the trip, how real it felt, how it had changed him. And suddenly, he knew exactly where he had to go to find the life he wanted. A place where he could just smile and make people happy.

CHAPTER FOUR

The Faithless Pastor

Thomas woke in the dark, his hand sliding across the sheet beside him. Cold linen. No warmth. Only emptiness. The same crushing void that pierced him every morning, relentless as a clock's ticking. The old, corrosive questions crept back, a familiar, bitter taste. He shoved them away and sat up. God's work demanded him, whether he was up for it or not.

In the kitchen, a mouse nestled in the oat tin, another one of Jimmy's presents. At least this one was dead. The last Thomas had encountered was scrambling between his sheets, leaving a breadcrumb trail behind as it fought to escape the freshly laundered bedding.

He never told his housekeeper about the offerings he found scattered around the house. If Connie knew how her son entertained himself living at the parsonage, the poor boy would be in for a walloping. Thomas wrapped up the mouse and ruined oats to hide the crime from her. Losing his breakfast was no matter. He hadn't felt like eating, anyway.

He dropped the body bag in a bin on his way next door. Even at this early hour, the air hung heavy, preparing for another scorcher. In the church hall, a handful of faithful had gathered for morning prayer.

Oh Lord, let my soul rise up to meet you as the day rises to meet the sun.

But Thomas's soul didn't rise. It sagged. Worn thin from shepherding his flock day after day in the heat of a Mississippi summer without his beloved wife to tether him in the quiet hours. *May she rest in peace.*

The ache of her absence gnawed as he set off to visit an elderly couple, housebound by frailty. He stocked their pantry with canned goods and cooked them the sausages meant for his own breakfast. A surge of nausea rose in his throat as the meat sizzled in the pan. Something was definitely off with his gut this morning. He kept his distance while the couple ate, then led them in prayer, hoping their faith would draw the grace of Jesus into their humble dwelling.

"Thank you, Pastor," said the husband, pulling himself up from a sunken armchair to see his guest out.

"Please don't trouble yourself," Thomas protested.

"No trouble." But it was. The hobble to the entrance took an age. When a supportive arm was offered, the old man waved it off, but Thomas said nothing. Sometimes, all a man had left was his pride.

The walk back to the hall for the weekly church meeting also dragged. Sweat streamed down his body as if it were midday, and by the time he arrived, his shirt was soaked through.

"You feelin' alright, Pastor?" asked a committee member.

"This heat'll do a man in," he replied, dabbing his

forehead with a large white handkerchief as he sat down at a folding table. There was no time to dwell on incidentals, his schedule was full. "Our first item of business this morning is great news: John's agreed to be baptized."

A wolf whistle. "Ain't he a little old for savin'?"

"It's never too late to come to Our Lord." But Thomas had also been surprised by the town drunk's sudden swerve toward God. In his experience, life chipped away at faith rather than built it. Yet the fact remained: come Sunday, he'd be dunking a fifty-nine-year-old convert in an inflatable swimming pool.

Talk turned from birth to death.

"My momma wants to be buried at Needmore."

He shivered at this ghost from the past. "We aren't allowed to place people in the ground there anymore."

"She wants to be with my daddy," the woman insisted. "Couldn't we sneak her into Odd Fellows?"

"I'm afraid not. The cemetery's been decommissioned." It wouldn't sit well with the town leaders and Thomas needed them onside to perform his work. He understood the urge, though. His own kin were buried in the old "Colored Cemetery," as the city once called it, unmarked and lost to history. He rubbed his forehead, a heaviness pressing behind his eyes.

Bible Study was next. With Easter on the horizon, the group revisited the resurrection of Jesus. Thomas let others lead as his headache thickened. His mind wandered until it snagged on a snippet of text. *Blessed are those who have not seen and yet believed.* Had this passage been chosen to taunt him? He gazed at the bowed heads around him. There was no doubt there, only devotion—faces aglow with love of the Lord. If only he could share in that ecstasy.

A wave of exhaustion crashed over him. After the final *amen,* he stumbled home, desperate for a moment's rest. Behind closed lids, the dark days of Needmore rose before him. Over the past decade, the area had been targeted for "urban renewal," shattering the African American sanctuary at the heart of town. Homes were torn down, long-standing residents displaced, and community bonds broken. Some families remained, but many drifted to the outskirts, where they scrambled to survive, bereft of their old support networks. He'd joined that exodus after his wife's passing, seeking solace for himself as much as for his flock.

An insistent ringing called him back to duty. The news on the phone was grim: a young woman in his church had been sexually assaulted. Why did God send such trials to good people? He'd wrestled with this question all his years of service, and still found no answer. Forcing himself up on weak legs, he set out for the hospital.

The woman he found in emergency was a shadow of the person he knew, unable to utter more than single words in response to his ministrations. The room spun as he contemplated her future: a legacy of bruises and broken bones, emotional scars, police questioning, and the inevitable whispers about the length of her dress and why she'd walked home alone. As if that excused anything. He saw his own crushing hopelessness mirrored in her eyes.

His whole body throbbed with pain by the time he returned home. The mother with six hungry children would have to wait, whatever devil beset him was more than heat exhaustion. He rifled through the medicine cupboard, but it was bare, a rare miss for his housekeeper. Of all the days for him to fall ill, why did it have to be her one day off this month? With no other choice, he rang the drugstore to place an order.

"The flu's been mighty bad this year," said Mercy.

"You think I got the flu?" He was too unwell to be polite.

"Headache and aches in your muscles? Sure sounds like it. I'll send my boy 'round with aspirin. That'll bring the fever down."

He collapsed onto the couch in the living room, too spent to do anything but await the delivery.

Of course it had to be Isaiah coming to his rescue—the last person he wanted to see in his weak state. That boy had caused quite a stir at church with his claim that the afterlife was one big party to which everyone was invited. He was spreading the Word, but of what? Utter blasphemy!

There'd been an *incident* a couple of months ago when a notoriously crotchety member of his congregation turned up one Sunday with a huge smile on his face. Thomas had burned through the service, desperate to learn what had sparked such a transformation.

"I been talkin' to Isaiah," the man had said, gripping Thomas's hand at the church door. "There's somethin' good waitin' for me on the other side."

Thomas's eyes narrowed. "What exactly did Isaiah say?"

"That we all get into heaven. Beats rottin' down here. I've stopped takin' those meds the doc gave me. Gonna let nature take its course."

"You can't do that!"

A curious look. "Why not? With my wife dead and buried, what am I hangin' on fer?"

"Your family."

The man snorted.

"Don't you let Isaiah think what he says is the living truth," Thomas pressed. "He needs to believe in that version of heaven, that's all. A boy feels the absence of a father more than ever when he's a teenager."

But the man only smirked and turned away.

Lying here now, eyes drooping with a heaviness he struggled to fight, Thomas felt that siren call himself. He wanted with his whole heart to believe his wife and unborn child had found salvation after pneumonia took them. Besides, who was he to call anyone out? He'd stood at gravesides proclaiming the hope of resurrection, talked of a heaven where death and suffering are no more—but he no longer believed his own words. Each Sunday he mounted the pulpit to preach the Word of God, knowing he was a fraud.

Shame kept him silent. To confess his doubts would be to fail in his mission.

His vision swam, the room tilting in slow, sickening waves. It was hard to say when the rot in his faith set in. When his wife and unborn child passed? When Mercy lost her husband? Only an unexpected job offer at the local drugstore had saved her and Isaiah from ruin. But few such stories ended well. Too many of his flock had been crushed under fate's wheel, dragged under by debt, or the law, or by being in the wrong place at the wrong time. Like the woman in hospital. She'd needed more than his empty words, just as he needed more than aspirin to heal right now.

Nausea surged up through his throat. What would Connie say if he threw up on the couch? He tried to stand and walk to the bathroom, but his muscles refused to obey, so he rolled onto the floorboards instead. One of her many cats padded across the room to lick his face. It did nothing to cool the fire that engulfed him. His body shivered uncontrollably, clothing clinging to his skin like a sodden shroud, limp as his faith.

"Uhhhhhh!" he yelled as his body churned and gave way.

Voices called out.

"Preacher? You here?"

"We got your medicine."

Jimmy and Isaiah. Why'd she have to send Jimmy too? As if he didn't feel humiliated enough lying in a pool of vomit and urine.

The living room door creaked open, and footsteps approached.

"The pastor don't look too good," said Isaiah.

"Stay back," said Jimmy, his voice several feet away. "We don't wanna catch anything."

"He needs help." A step closer. "We have your medicine...Pastor Thomas?"

"Y-ee-s?" A tiny croak through cracked lips.

"Shall we leave the bottle for you?"

Thomas's mouth refused to open again.

"What we gonna do?" Isaiah's voice trembled with panic.

"I'll get my momma." Footsteps, then the slam of the front door.

The living room window slid open. "Jimmy! JIMMY! Don't leave me here alone with him."

The singing of bicycle wheels faded away.

A sigh, then footsteps near Thomas's head again. "You okay, Pastor? Don't worry...angels are watching over you."

That boy made up all sorts of nonsense. "I know you believe, son, but I see only darkness."

"That's cause your eyes are closed," Isaiah insisted.

Thomas opened them. "Still dark...Oh...Wait!" He rode his breath out like a wave and found himself flying through a star-filled expanse, his body stretched out—a vast, shifting cloud, endless and serene. Ahead pulsed a huge white light, drawing him in.

You are a child of God!

The words reverberated through him.

Then he plunged into the sphere.

Pain and turmoil melted away, thawed by a tremendous warmth that washed over him. With every fiber of his being he knew he was deeply loved. It was a knowing beyond reason, the deepest sense of peace he'd ever experienced. He felt held in God's mercy.

We love you! Why don't you have more fun? Lighten up! Life is meant to be joyful. A soft giggle threaded through these words.

His throat tightened as stars stretching into the farthest corners of the cosmos twinkled at him.

Another voice murmured in the far distance.

"*Bless the Lord...who heals all your diseases...and redeems your life from the pit...with...with steadfast love and mercy.*"

Isaiah was praying—making a meal of the psalm, as he did every other aspect of scripture. Yet an unexpected tenderness rose within Thomas for this fatherless child. The boy clearly needed someone to guide him into manhood.

Deep in his soul, he knew he faced a choice: remain in the light or return to Earth. He didn't want to leave. Why miss the chance to see his family again? Yet even as he thought this, he pictured Isaiah waiting alone by his body and recalled the haunted eyes of the woman in hospital. Who would walk with her through the shadows ahead if he abandoned her now? His work wasn't complete. Perhaps it had only just begun.

The light dissolved.

Isaiah's muttering swelled in his ears.

Weight crashed back into him.

He gasped, air rushing into his lungs. His body ached but no longer burned—the fever had eased. A strange calm settled over him. He was alive. And what a joyous gift that was.

More footsteps.

"He had any medicine?" asked a familiar voice.

"No, ma'am," Isaiah replied. "He couldn't—"

"Out of my way...Head up and open your mouth, Preacher. I'm going to give you something that'll set you right."

There was no refusing that voice, even for a pastor on his deathbed. A spoonful of something thick and foul slid over his tongue. He gagged and opened his eyes. "What...what is that?"

"Castor oil," said Connie, twisting the lid back on the bottle. "Did me the world of good when I was in labor."

Thomas did something he'd never done before. He spat on the floor. "I'm not having a baby. Where's the aspirin?"

She placed a hand on his forehead. "No need for that. You don't have a fever."

"Then why?"

She shook the spoon at him like a schoolmistress scolding a truant. "Castor oil's good for everything. My daddy swore by it."

He swallowed his protest. There was no arguing with his housekeeper once she brought her dearly departed father into the conversation.

Jimmy stepped out of her shadow. "How you feeling, Preacher?"

"Mighty fine, child, mighty fine," said Thomas, easing himself up against the couch.

Connie took in the pool of filth on the floor. "It don't look like you're fine."

"I've been in the presence of Our Lord."

"Hallelujah!" shouted Isaiah, his face radiant.

"What a load of bull," Jimmy mumbled.

Connie clipped her boy across the ears.

"Ow!" Jimmy rubbed his head. "What was that for?"

"Why'd you wait so long to get me?" she scolded.

He opened and shut his mouth several times. Thomas knew it would have been hard for the boy to locate his mother while she was collecting rents across town. That he'd found her at all was another one of God's miracles—though Thomas doubted the Almighty would have insisted on the castor oil.

A man with a bulging bag rushed in. He gave Connie the briefest nod before hurrying to Thomas's side. "I hear tell you've taken ill, Pastor. Let me tend to you at once."

"No need," Thomas said, levering himself up. "I'm a newborn man."

"Don't you go getting carried away," Connie warned. "You looked like death warmed over when I walked in."

Ignoring his housekeeper, he turned to Isaiah. "You took real good care of me, son."

"I'm sure he did," said the doctor, offering the boy a warm smile.

Isaiah didn't appear to hear them. His gaze was fixed on Jimmy, who twirled a finger near his ear, mocking the pastor's sanity. Thomas watched the spark in Isaiah's eyes flicker, then vanish, replaced by something hard. What damage had that simple gesture done?

He had no chance to find out as Connie bustled him off to bed—not that day, nor any day that followed. From then on, Isaiah kept his head down in church and bolted the moment service ended, always in Jimmy's wake. Every attempt Thomas made to reach out was met with rejection. Nor did the boy speak of heaven again. Yet this wasn't the source of relief he'd expected. On the contrary, unease took root. The light had returned to his own life, but a darkness had entered Isaiah, and he could do nothing to shift it. Whatever guidance the lad sought on his path into manhood now lay beyond God's reach.

CHAPTER FIVE

The Estranged Daughter

Aisha waited behind the wheel of her car. And waited. And waited. Her legs jiggled against the cheap plastic seat of the rental car, itching to stand and stretch, to shake off the tension coiled in her muscles. But she didn't dare move from her hiding place.

Eventually, a familiar figure appeared on a side road. And another. A middle-aged man and an elderly woman shuffled closer. His swarthy features were obscured beneath a jet-black mustache and beard. She was veiled from head to toe in a loose garment, with only her face visible.

Twenty meters away.

Ten.

Five.

Aisha shrank back in her seat, picked up the newspaper she'd bought at the airport that morning—the largest broadsheet on sale—and raised it before her face, peering through a small pinprick she'd pierced in the middle. The man and woman didn't look around, didn't even talk to one another. Their stares vacant, the woman's hand resting lightly on his slack arm, they entered a nearby vehicle without comment.

After their car exited the security gate, Aisha made her move, retracing their footsteps toward a one-story building. She peered through the glass doors at the entrance. The nurse at reception had his head down.

Taking a deep breath, she slipped inside, diving down a corridor before he had time to look up. Orange doors opened left and right onto strangers wrapped in hospital bedding. An empty room with a rope of tasbih beads on the bedside table looked promising, but there was no sign of her mother.

Aisha swallowed a lump in her throat. Was she too late? She had no choice but to inquire at the front desk.

"Excuse me?"

The nurse looked up and smiled. "How can I help you?"

"I'm looking for Fatima Ahmadi."

"And you are?"

"Her daughter, Aisha."

The smile faded. "There's no daughter on the visitor list."

She'd prepared for this possibility.

"I have proof." She pulled a crumpled family photo out of her handbag, downloaded years ago from a relative's Facebook page and stuffed in a bottom drawer, where she'd sneak the odd peek in rare bursts of nostalgia. The nurse studied it, hesitating, clearly wondering about their family estrangement and whether her mother would want to see her. She could only hope the circumstances of this hospital stay pushed his decision in her favor.

At last, he slid the photo back. "Your mother's in the Reflective Garden. Wait here until I find someone to take you." He still didn't trust her.

A harried aide appeared after ten minutes to hurry her out the unit's back door and across the corridor into a small garden. At a glass table sat a lone figure muttering over a tattered book. Aisha scowled at her mother's veiled head. Even at death's door, the woman still donned her hijab, an emblem of her lifelong submission.

She cleared her throat. "Hey, Mum."

"Aisha?" Red-rimmed eyes widened. "Aisha!"

Hands reached out, but she didn't return the gesture. "Is this a good time for me to visit?"

Her mother beamed. "It is always good when I see you, my daughter. Allah has answered my prayers. You are here!" She spoke in her native tongue. Her grasp of English had never been strong and had perhaps faded with illness. Aisha's Kurdish was rusty, but she tried to reciprocate.

"Are you...expecting anyone?"

"Your father and grandmother have left."

"I assume Dad's driving Nene home. Will he be back soon?" She threw a nervous glance at the door behind her.

"He will come back tomorrow."

The tension that had filled her body since she'd exited her car fell away.

Her mother beckoned. "Come closer, I want to see you."

She slipped onto the opposite wooden bench, faded and splintered by the sun's harsh rays. Her mother's eyes stayed fixed on her face—as if she were a drink to quench an overwhelming thirst.

"You've cut your hair. Dyed it," she observed.

"I had to. You know that." Aisha could taste the bitterness on her tongue.

An approving nod. "Red suits you."

"Um, thanks." She pondered this transgression. Her mother, daring to approve an act they both knew her father would not.

"How did you know I was here?" her mother asked.

"I still have contacts in our community," she snapped. "Did you think I'd been banished completely?"

Her mother's lips pressed together.

"A school friend told me you had breast cancer," she continued.

"It has spread through my body."

"I'm sorry." It was a knee-jerk response. *I'm sorry for your loss. I'm sorry you're about to lose your life.* As if she weren't related to this person. As if her mother weren't a once-beloved parent. Fury remained her dominant emotion.

"I'm not." Her mother smiled. "You've come back."

"I wasn't sure I'd be welcome."

"Allah sent you to me. I'm blessed!" Arms stretched wide as if to invite her inside, but she remained on the far side of the table.

"How long have you been in care?" she asked.

"A few weeks. It's where you come when..." Her mother didn't finish. She didn't have to. Aisha could read the death sentence in the stooped posture and gray skin.

"Did you have far to travel?" her mother asked.

"I can't let you know where I live. You'd tell Dad."

A nod.

Aisha sighed. "I hope he's taking good care of you. You've spent almost your entire life looking after him." Married at fourteen, her mum had put up with too much for the last forty years. "How often does he visit?"

"He brings his mother every day. She wants to make sure the staff are looking after me."

"I bet she does! Tells you what to eat? What to wear? Encourages you to hurry home, so she doesn't have to look after Dad and the boys herself?"

"She can only stay an hour each day. Your father must go to work."

A laugh choked in Aisha's throat. "No wonder you checked into this place. There's no escaping her criticism at home."

"I'm grateful to them both."

Aisha's teeth ground together. Her mother's forbearance had always rubbed her the wrong way. In her own experience, yelling, screaming and kicking down walls were the only ways to improve your lot in life. Sometimes, you even had to burn everything to the ground and start again to get what you deserved. But even at this late hour, her mother looked for her reward in a dusty book.

"How did you find out about the cancer?" she asked.

"There was a lump in my breast." Her mother was matter of fact, as if this was a normal occurrence, or perhaps, the will of Allah.

"And you saw a doctor?"

"After a few months."

Aisha's voice sharpened. "Why didn't you go to a medical clinic straight away?"

"I couldn't get there by myself."

"Dad wouldn't drive you?"

"He was busy."

Aisha's jaw clenched. What was wrong with her family? "Have you heard of Uber, Mum?"

A shrug. "I don't have money for whatever that is."

"Dad gives you housekeeping funds."

"He gives it to Nene."

Aisha scoffed. "How do you pay for groceries, then?"

"I take your grandmother with me wherever I go."

Her breath caught. "Oh, Mum! I never saw...didn't know that you were trapped too."

Her mother's hands found hers. "You were busy living your life."

"I guess I was." But it didn't feel like enough of an excuse. How could she have missed the signs of her mother's subjugation?

"As you should be."

Another blasphemy. Her mother must be really near the end to lose self-control like this. Or maybe being on her own for the first time in her life had loosened her tongue. "Have my brothers been to see you?"

"Once or twice. Tariq rang from jail, which was nice."

"I bet!" It was hard to keep the sarcasm out of her voice.

"None of my children has led an easy life." Grief was written on her mother's face as a shared history passed silently between them.

Aisha's parents had fled to Australia as refugees expecting sanctuary, but found only hostility—all for the color of their skin and the way they dressed. In Iraq, her father had been highly respected, but in Melbourne, he could only get a lowly position on a factory floor, where he was endlessly taunted for being a 'wog', a foreigner excluded from comradeship.

"They show me no respect," he constantly complained. "Call me a dog! Even though I work longer and harder than any of them." His outbursts seeped into the walls of their fibro house until it vibrated with his resentment.

Her brothers had endured the same treatment: bullied at school, harassed in pubs, and questioned like criminals. So, in time, that's what they became. Tariq, the eldest, fell first, drawing Husam in as his right-hand man. Kaseem hesitated, steered briefly by a caring teacher, but when hope clashed with reality, he joined the crew. Khadim, the youngest, simply did what he was told.

Aisha, born last, gave as good as she got in the

schoolyard and earned her peer's respect. Her childhood blossomed with friendships that introduced her to a different world to the one inhabited by her family—the root of their eventual separation.

"I've missed you," her mother said, softly.

"Well, whose fault is that?"

"It was the will of Allah!"

Aisha bit back the scream rising in her chest.

Her mother had stayed silent when her father arranged for her to be married off to a man back in the old country. She'd been in Year 9, powerless to prevent this plan from going ahead. Her large group of friends—and secret Aussie boyfriend, Cody—could do nothing. Despite her pleas for a chance at a different life, her father had remained resolute. Nor had her tears moved her mother to intervene.

"What can I do?" she'd replied with a shrug during their private conversations.

"Talk to him!"

"He won't listen."

She'd known her mother was right, but resented her nonetheless.

Only her own desperation had saved her. A last-minute confession to the high school counselor led to police intervention. Social services arranged accommodation when she was banished from her family. After word on the street got out that her brothers were seeking retribution, she'd been moved to a safe house and eventually provided with a new identity.

There was no possibility of returning to the family fold. Not with her brothers' criminal links. Not when Tariq had sworn to make her pay for dishonoring their name. But she had no intention of going up in flames. Her only comfort was that Cody came with her into the strange new life chosen by the justice system, giving up his own loving family to stay by her side. Another crime committed by those who were meant to love her—one too great ever to forgive.

Her mother's fingers lingered on the edge of her Qur'an, tracing the gilded margin as though drawing strength from the words inside. "Have you spoken with your brothers?"

"Why would I? They want me dead. As far as they're concerned, I brought shame on my family."

"They are the ones who brought shame on us," her mother whispered.

It shocked Aisha—this defiance.

"Your father says nothing," her mother went on, "but I know his head hangs low because of them."

"He never said."

"The shame runs deep, where there are no words."

This knowledge wasn't balm enough for her wounds. "Leaving broke me, Mum. Tore me in two. There was Aisha before, with a family, and Aisha after, an orphan. It took a long time to put myself back together again."

"I was happy for you."

"Happy I broke?"

"Happy you broke away. Found your path. I prayed

for that. You wanted a different life and wouldn't have fought so hard for it if less had been asked of you."

Another transgression. A welcome one.

Aisha swallowed. "Prayer can't fix every trauma."

While her Muslim beliefs had been cast aside as she fully embraced her new identity as a true-blue Aussie sheila, she hadn't escaped her heritage completely. A crone flashing a knife had haunted her dreams since childhood. Cody was the one who discovered the damage between her legs. She'd pursued every medical option, seeking to restore what had been stolen from her, but no one could mend her broken nerves. You could leave tradition behind, but it never quite left you.

Yet prayer remained her mother's answer to everything.

"Will you take me to the chapel?" she asked.

Aisha searched the garden for the aide, but she'd disappeared. "Am I allowed?"

"It's my last request."

"You mean, of me?" It made sense. She had no reason to be back this way again.

It was a slow, stop-start journey, with many hesitations on her mother's part, and a few quiet queries on her own about whether her mother wouldn't be better off back in bed. There wasn't much left of her, just a slight weight in Aisha's arms. As soon as they entered the tiny chapel, her mother sank to her knees.

A whispered request. "Pray with me."

Aisha crossed her arms. "Faith and I parted ways a long time ago."

"Please!"

She sighed. "Fine... if I must." She lowered herself onto the carpet.

Time ticked by. Her knees tired first.

"I should get you back." She helped her mother upright, earning a radiant smile in return.

"The Prophet has promised he'll watch over you."

She snorted softly. "Hmm! Can he whistle up transport to get you back to your room as well?"

Her mother nodded. "He always looks after us."

As they turned into the corridor, Aisha stopped short. A wheelchair sat abandoned outside the doorway. To her relief, her mother made no comment on its miraculous appearance. But for a moment, even she wondered if Allah did, in fact, provide.

Back in the room, her mother collapsed onto the bed and shrank into herself as Aisha adjusted the covers.

"Are you alright, Mum?"

A faint smile. "I waited for *you*."

She stiffened. "But you didn't know I was coming."

"Allah promised you would. I needed to look upon you one more time."

"Don't say that!" Despite her anger, Aisha didn't want to be reminded of her mother's condition.

"I can go home now."

"But shouldn't you stay in hospital?"

A long sigh was the only response.

She leaned in close and whispered, "Are you scared?"

"Living is scary. Not death. The Prophet will welcome me."

Aisha place her hand on an upturned palm on the bed covers. "You haven't had much of a life, have you, Mum?"

"I have you here—my greatest blessing—and my sons."

"You still love us?"

She gave a faint nod.

"After everything?" Aisha pressed.

Her mother's chin trembled. "I forgive you."

The word hit Aisha like a slap. Not for its cruelty, but for the unbearable grace of it.

She spluttered. "W-what?"

"Maybe one day," her mother whispered, voice thinning, "you can find it in your heart to forgive *me*... You may look different, but you're still...my Aisha."

"That trip to the prayer room was too much for you, Mum. You should rest."

"Allah Hafiz!" said her mother, staring straight at her.

Aisha didn't need God's protection—she had her own wits for that—but she accepted the blessing nonetheless.

Her mother's gaze lifted to the ceiling.

"He has come."

"Who?"

"The Prophet."

"You can see him?"

A nod. "He will watch over you and your daughters."

Aisha froze. "How do you know I have daughters?"

"He told me you have two."

Her pulse quickened. "Maybe. Maybe not."

"Are they happy?"

An image rose of two girls laughing in the Gold Coast surf, Cody standing watch nearby, steady as a rock. Not like her.Always on high alert, waiting for the tap on the shoulder, for the hit to come.

"Yes, they're happy." She chewed her bottom lip. "Can you ask The Prophet if they'll stay safe?"

Her mother cocked an ear. "He says yes."

Aisha remained in the room for a few more minutes, but her mother said no more.

As she headed for the entrance, the nurse at the desk called after her, "Shall I send an aide to collect your mother from the garden?"

She stopped mid-stride and turned. "Mum's in bed."

"What?"

"I brought her back from the prayer room."

"She went to the prayer room?" His voice rose a notch. "In a wheelchair?"

"No, we walked."

The nurse stood, disbelief flaring. "There and back?"

"Just there."

He started jogging toward her mother's room. "Fatima hasn't walked anywhere for weeks."

She ran after him. Though he tried to block her view, she glimpsed her mother's eyes—wide open, a look of pure bliss on her face.

"She said she'd found the strength to move on. I... I thought she meant..."

Sitting in the airport later, she caught the faintest trace of a familiar perfume, heavy and musky. Gooseflesh rippled down her arms. She knew her mother was there, holding her in a silence that needed no words.

For a long moment, she simply sat with it: the warmth, the knowing, the quiet.

Regret clawed at her ribs. Her daughters would never know their grandmother's love; fierce in its pride, sudden in its softness. But the ache gradually eased into something else. She drew in a breath and let it out slowly. That love was still here, threaded through her. She could carry it forward, not as a wound but as a legacy.

As the boarding call sounded, she rose, lighter than she'd felt in years. The past had settled, and two souls had finally found peace. First, her mother. Then herself.

CHAPTER SIX

The Resentful Son

Ọdẹwálé blew lazy rings of smoke up toward the branches of the ìrókò tree above, the scent of igbó thick on the humid air. Then he passed the joint to his cousin, stretched out beside him on the dry earth.

"I've missed you, brother."

Ọlá took a long drag before responding. "How's life here?"

Ọdẹwálé let out a half-laugh. "Baba won't let me breathe.

Everything with him is tight, tight. Like he wants to fry me in a pot that can't contain me."

"He still wants you to be a hunter?"

"We quarreled again before he left for the forest yesterday." The memory stung. He could still hear his father's voice, deep, commanding, and impossible to ignore.

"You are like the divine spirit Obàtálá," Baba had said, pacing the compound. "Drunk on your own ideas. Obàtálá failed to form the world, though the task was given to him. You too will fail if you refuse the counsel of our ancestors. You have much to learn, ọmọ mi."

My dear child! The phrase always came like a soft

slap, both love and rebuke. But he'd stood his ground.

"Our ways need to change, Baba. We'll fall behind the Ìgbò if we don't embrace technology."

"Do not fall into the trap of comparing our people to other tribes," his father said. "When the white man drew his lines on a map, he did not ask whose land was whose. He joined us together in ways that are not natural. The Yoruba know something deeper; it is not technology that brings success, it is education. Our people rise wherever they go. The most influential Nigerians in the world are Yoruba. We lead in politics, we prosper in wealth, and our sons and daughters sit in the governments of the strongest nations."

"Because we are sycophants to the powers-that-be," he shot back.

"Because we are taught to be respectful," his father corrected. "That is why we rise where others fall."

"But most of our people are poor, Baba."

His father shook his head. "What is this poverty you speak of? Do we not eat? Do we not laugh? Are we not rich in spirit?"

He folded his arms. "I don't believe in that spirit talk."

"Be careful, Olùfẹ́ mi," said his father softly. "Our ancestors are listening."

Olùfẹ́ mi! Ọdẹwálé did not feel beloved. Not when his father refused to hear him out.

At eighteen, he was a man by every standard that mattered: old enough to think for himself and to choose his own future. This was a new world, and his people needed to face it head-on. The old stories wouldn't buy you a Tecno phone or a Dell laptop. They couldn't connect you to the world beyond the village. To him, the future lived on screens, in glowing symbols that linked one person to another across oceans. In that world, no one cared about spirits or ancestral laws. All that mattered was signal strength and who was online. His resolve to carve his own path hardened like sunbaked clay.

"Here you go, bro."

Ọlá passed the joint back, dragging Ọdẹwálé out of his thoughts. Anger eased as the smoke warmed his chest. "Ah-ah! This thing strong o. You bring am from the city?"

"Ehen!" Ọlá grinned. "Better than the igbó we get around here. I fit bring you one full suitcase next time."

Ọdẹwálé turned to stare at his cousin. "Suitcase? How much money you don make, sef?"

"Twenty thousand."

"Naira?" he asked, naming the Nigerian currency.

Ọlá burst out laughing. "Naira ke? Dollars, my guy. Fresh from the white man's land."

Ọdẹwálé's eyes widened. Twenty thousand dollars could buy plenty of phones and computers.

"Those American women get money like water," Ọlá boasted.

Ọdẹwálé grinned. "Maybe I should become a Yahoo boy."

Ọlá drew on the joint and exhaled slowly. "E no be

for everybody, my guy. You gats do plenty research to act like another person. And you need patience to build trust. To sweet-talk a foreign woman no be beans."

Ọdẹwálé pictured the thin, blonde sticks he'd seen on television in Lagos. Their tight faces and forced smiles. Americans always looked worried. He didn't want to get tangled in their problems through a screen. Women with meat on their bones and laughter in their eyes suited him better. Besides, that kind of hustle wasn't meant for him.

"Baba no go gree if I follow your path," he murmured.

Ọlá clicked his tongue. "He should be happy sef. If you turn Yahoo boy, he can finally rest. We be the new kings in this country, my guy. Think of the money you fit send home. Baba no go need to dey hunt again."

They kept talking, trading jokes about Lagos girls and fast cash, until their stomachs began to rumble.

Ọlá pushed to his feet, palmed the joint into a tree hollow, then grinned. "Make we go raid your mama kitchen. I sure say she get vegetable soup for her long-lost nephew."

Ọdẹwálé hesitated. "Baba go ask questions." Then he sighed and stood. "But I dey hungry. Make we go."

On the village outskirts, an elder stood shading his eyes with one hand as he scanned the horizon. When he spotted Ọdẹwálé, he hurried forward.

The cousins bowed their heads as he approached.

"You must come at once," the elder said, his voice tight with urgency.

Ọdẹwálé frowned. This was not the way traditional greetings began.

"Good evening," he said, unwilling to let go of the expected forms in case he got into more trouble. "What's the hurry?"

"There's been an accident. Your father is asking for you. He..." The man's words faltered. "You'll see. Come."

A crowd pressed around the meeting hut at the village center, faces turned toward whatever was happening inside.

"Quickly!" someone shouted.

"Your father is calling for you," another urged.

Ọdẹwálé was swept forward by many hands beneath the thatched roof. The scent of packed earth closed around him, cutting through the fog in his head. Something serious had happened to his father. He could feel it in the silence beneath the noise. The anger he carried dissolved into icy fear. He lingered at the edge of the throng, unwilling to see what waited within.

A weak voice called out.

"Ọ-dẹ-wálé?"

The gathering parted, forcing him to step forward. He knelt before the mat in the room's center, touching his forehead to the earth. When he raised his eyes, an ugly scene lay before him. His father—the man who had nimbly danced around lions and leopards and elephants—lay utterly savaged. A massive, blood-slicked rupture slashed across his belly, running deep through flesh and muscle, his insides reduced to pulp. The wound shone crimson and raw, glistening as red as the earth beneath their feet.

Ọdẹwálé swallowed. "Greetings, Baba."

"Greetings, ọmọ mi! Are you well?"

"Yes, I am well. And...you?"

His father smiled faintly and touched his chest. "As you see, I fought a boar and the beast won."

Ọdẹwálé glanced at his mother, who was praying softly nearby. He didn't need to ask about his father's fate. Grief was written in her eyes.

"It is time," said his father.

He shivered. "Time for what?"

"For you to take my place."

"Baba, how can I do that when you are still here?"

His father's voice softened. "My time on this earth is almost over, ọmọ mi. You must take up my mantle: become an Ọdẹ."

A vein pulsed on Ọdẹwálé's forehead. Even now, on his deathbed, his father was applying pressure.

"Why do you want me to take up the old ways, Baba?" he whispered. "Look at what hunting did to you."

His father glanced down at the oozing gash on his chest.

"I am proud of this wound, Ọdẹwálé, as I am proud of every mark on my body. Each one is proof of my work as a provider for this tribe. It is an honor to be a hunter, no matter what darkness crosses your path. The forest tests a man's courage: every path hiding its own teeth. But a true Ọdẹ learns to walk with both fear and pride in his quiver. I have been blessed to belong to such an ancient and noble calling."

"It gets you killed!"

"As do motors, which you young people love so much to

drive." A weak smile touched his father's lips. "Do not trouble yourself with my passing. A man's moment of death is mapped out from birth. Nothing and no one can change that. But the long tradition of hunting in our family rests in your hands. These skills have passed from father to first son since Ògún walked the earth. You must follow in my footsteps."

"But...I—"

"Promise me this!"

Whispers echoed through the hut.

"He cannot refuse his father's request!"

"Young ones do not respect authority anymore."

"You're right! They don't have a single fuck to give, as they like to say."

Ọdẹwálé's eyes blazed. The man he'd looked up to all his life was leaving this world without accepting his ideas, and worse, binding him to an unwanted destiny as his final wish.

But what choice did he have?

"I... I'll give it a try."

Murmurs of approval broke out behind him.

There was some consolation in his capitulation.

Becoming a hunter would lend him an aura of authority; perhaps then someone might listen to his ideas. But even as the thought formed, he sensed the cost—something vast was being surrendered to finally be heard. His throat tightened, a hollow ache spreading through his chest.

He bent close to his father's ear. "Must you leave, Baba?"

His father closed his eyes briefly, as though listening for something beyond the hut. Then he spoke. "This is how it was meant to be. Take comfort; my spirit will not fade away. I will transition into a new life, and one day return as a newborn child. Maybe your firstborn, if the Creator wills it."

Ọdẹwálé leaned closer. "But Baba, I don't believe in any of that."

His father's fingers searched for his hand, and when they found it, gave the slightest squeeze. "I will give you a sign to show the truth of my words. You will know." A breath shuddered through him. Half sigh, half release. He said no more.

For hours, the only sounds were prayer and muffled sniffling. The women sat close to the mat, their low voices threading soft "Àmín" through the air each time someone murmured a blessing. A bowl of water was placed by the entrance, a sprig of ewé akòko herbs floating inside, ready to wash the body when the end came.

Ọdẹwálé knew what would come later. After the mourning, the rituals, and the burial, there would be drumming, dancing, and feasting to celebrate his father's reunion with the ancestors. Ògún's praise songs would rise with the smoke of cooking fires, and the men would pour palm wine to the earth in libation. A swell of pride filled his chest: nobody knew how to throw a party like the Yoruba. But now, as the light in his father's eyes dimmed, the weight of imminent loss filled the hut with soft weeping.

Near dawn, his father's eyes widened, and stillness settled over his broken frame. Somewhere outside, a night bird cried and fell silent. The air thickened, heavy with waiting; even the crickets paused their song. Time itself seemed to hold its breath.

Ọdẹwálé fixed his gaze on the old man's face, willing him to breathe again. A faint scent of camwood drifted through the air, warm and woody. Then a shimmer near his father's head.

Ọdẹwálé blinked. *He's coming back to us!* The thought collapsed before it could fully form. *No... that isn't him.*

Something luminous and weightless unfurled from the crown of his father's head and lingered in the air, almost translucent. His father's likeness gazed down at him, the warmth of his presence filling the hut with love. Ọdẹwálé closed his eyes, opened them again, then shook his head to clear the vision. Around him, the air filled with wailing as women's voices rose in songs of farewell. Only he seemed to see what hovered above, the spirit his father had become.

Was it real?

Did the self continue after death?

Had Baba been right all along?

Something inside him loosened—the same part that had clenched every time his father spoke of gods and ancestors. It wasn't belief he felt now, but knowing. The ice around his heart melted.

"Má bínú, Baba," he whispered. *Forgive me.*

His father smiled and reached upward, as if grasping unseen hands, before drifting through the thatched roof into the dawning light.

In that moment, Ọdẹwálé understood what his father had been trying to teach him and vowed to find another path forward, one that embraced the new while honoring his promise. There had to be a way that allowed room for both: the pulse of the modern world and the heartbeat of the old.

His shoulders straightened.

He would find that balance.

Whatever it took.

CHAPTER SEVEN

The Optimistic Good-For-Nothing

She had to die. It was the only solution. But Jimmy sure wished his mother would hurry up and do it. He'd been sitting by her bedside for weeks, playing the devoted son. And still she lingered, a frail, withered leech draining his inheritance.

He shot a sour look around the room, at the glossy floors, the soft lighting, the cheerful posters nobody believed. Care at this assisted living facility didn't come cheap. He didn't know the exact figures—she'd never let him anywhere near her finances—but judging by the look of the joint, whatever she was paying was too damn much. For the umpteenth time, he cursed the day she'd signed up to stay here before losing her mind.

However, her extended stay here had one silver lining: he hadn't had to look after her since the dementia diagnosis. Visiting was stressful enough. She either couldn't remember who he was—which was embarrassing—or she did. Also embarrassing. Either way, she spent most of their time together cussing at him. It was a relief that she'd been silenced, the fountain of foul words finally switched off.

It was the pet policy that had sold her on the place: cats were welcome. One lay under the crook of her arm now, taunting him with its smug proximity. He'd never been allowed that close. Affection was something his mother rationed, and never for him. In her eyes, he'd always been the wrong kind of child—too loud, too bold, too quick to run.

"Shoo!" he hissed, flapping his arms. The cat didn't budge. It knew its place in the pecking order.

He flopped back against his chair. Never mind. Its reign would end soon enough. This latest bout of pneumonia should finish his mother off. They'd moved her to the nursing wing, a sure sign the end was near. She certainly looked dead enough, her body a motionless lump beneath the covers.

Except, of course, for that damn stare.

It was unnerving the way her half-lidded eyes seemed to track his every move, as if the old woman were still judging him. He'd felt her tongue's sting his whole life. When would it stop? He was tired, bone-tired, and longed for the peace that would come when he no longer had to brace for her next blow.

To keep his distance from that gaze, he shoved his chair up against the window, watching for attractive women paying dutiful visits to their own decrepit relatives. He'd hit on one or two to break up the tedium of this death watch and even lined up a date for when "his grief had passed." He hoped the woman wouldn't be too scandalized if he recovered quickly, say in a week or two.

If only his mother would die.

He glanced back at the bed. She still looked like death warmed over. The temptation to shove her over the edge made his fingers itch. He scanned the room again for hidden cameras. You never knew, the nurses might smile at him, but you couldn't trust anyone these days. No lenses blinked at him. Yet he couldn't risk acting on the urge to silence her. With one pillow pressed over her face, his inheritance could be lost forever. And that damn money was the only thing standing between him and ruin.

Nothing ever worked out for him. Despite his many money-making schemes, somehow he always ended up with egg on his face, and often on the wrong side of the law. Cheap TVs he sold off the back of his pickup turned out to be stolen. Insurance schemes he peddled were never quite what they claimed. Even when he tried to go straight, taking a lousy job pumping gas and swearing things would be different, the owner turned out to have links to a local crime network; the place shut down overnight in a police raid. But this constant misfortune hadn't dampened his enthusiasm. He always had a plan to improve his life—many, in fact—and soon he'd be able to fund them.

When she finally bit that dust.

A warm weight brushed against his shin, another of her interminable cats. He lashed out with a kick, catching its fat belly just enough to send it scampering.

"Get away from me!"

He was sick of these vermin. She'd always treated them better than she'd treated him. *Her own son.* After a lifetime of being shoved aside, his inheritance was nothing less than his due.

A shapely figure outside the window caught his eye. Another prospective conquest. He flashed her a smile, and a look of triumph flickered across her face. *No...surely not.* Then the small child beside her came into focus. She tugged him along toward the entrance.

What the hell? How had she found him?

He bolted for the door, but it was too late. She was already marching down the corridor with one of the nurses. His gaze darted around the room. There was only one option. He threw the cat off the bed, yanked back the sheet, and pressed his body against the motionless form of his mother. It wasn't the first time he'd used this hiding place.

Footsteps entered the room.

"Where is he?" she demanded. "I saw him through the window a moment ago."

"Are you sure?" asked a familiar voice.

Jimmy scowled. Just his luck that Isaiah had grown up to work here.

"Yes," she snapped. "He must be here somewhere."

At the screech of the bathroom door, a silent laugh rose in his chest. He'd been caught holed up in there by a creditor once and had learned his lesson. Nobody outwitted Jimmy Moore twice.

A heavy weight slammed into his stomach. One of those blasted cats had leapt onto the bed and was circling on top of him, growling as if to give him away. Someone yanked it off, but not before it scored a jagged line across his stomach. His skin burned where the claws had raked him. It took every ounce of willpower not to cry out.

"Are you missing her, little buddy?" Isaiah cooed.

Jimmy's scowl deepened. That goody-two-shoes was probably cradling the beast in his arms and stroking its fur, like the perfect little boy he'd always been.

"I wanna go home, Momma," sang a childish voice.

"Don't you wanna meet your daddy?"

A foot stomped. "I. Wanna. Go. Home."

Jimmy grinned beneath the sheet. *That's my boy.*

Then a whisper of something he didn't want to name tugged at his chest. That was *his* boy.

A weary sigh. "Okay, honey. We'll come back."

The door slammed, but he stayed hidden for as long as he could bear it. When he finally emerged, it was with the wary caution of a snail poking out of its shell. He crawled across the floor to peer out the window, making sure his ex-wife was nowhere in sight before standing up. Her threat still rang in his ears. *She'd be back.* He'd have to keep his guard up from now on.

Dragging his chair over to his mother's bed, he wedged it behind the nightstand so no one could see him from outside.

His mother's dead-eyed stare met his.

"I know!" he snapped. "You don't approve. Tell me something new."

Her eyes continued to bore into him—just like they used to at the preacher's house the moment there was even a whiff of trouble. There'd been no salvation for him under that roof. Not from her. Nor from their so-called benefactor, Pastor Thomas. That sanctimonious snake-oil salesman made his skin crawl. His only joy as a boy came from messing with the man every chance he got. And the icing on the cake? He'd never been caught. The preacher had been too stupid to pick up on his tricks.

Jimmy leaned toward his mother, his voice low and bitter. "Why'd you stay so long with the preacher? You didn't have to. Not after you'd built up that portfolio of rental properties. We could have left. Lived like kings. But no, you kept working for that man until you were too sick to hide your illness. Why? Why, why, why?"

He felt a dark surge of pleasure, his tongue finally off the leash, releasing words he'd been saving a lifetime—the same savage joy he'd felt striding out the door on his eighteenth birthday, free at last. Still, he wasn't one to look a gift horse in the mouth, and he'd continued to rely on the preacher's protection every time a scheme blew up in his face. Debt collectors didn't knock on a pastor's door. And women seeking paternity support were too intimidated by the church to come calling. The preacher had been his unwitting savior time and time again. More fool him.

But he wouldn't need that old man's help anymore. His ship was about to come in. At last. The only thing he'd thank God for was that. He rubbed his hands together, already calculating the rent hikes he'd slap on his tenants. He'd be rolling in dough.

Once his mother got out of the way, that is.

His mind turned to the celebrations he'd treat himself to on that sweet, sweet day. Judging from her ashen complexion, it wouldn't be long now. So why wait? Maybe there was a mini bottle of champagne in the vending machine, just waiting for an occasion like this. And if not, that was a business idea he could pursue with his new funding. Not for retirement homes—far too dreary to ever set foot in again—but in birthing suites, a machine like that might make a killing.

Whistling under his breath, he set off down the corridor in search of refreshments.

The sight of Isaiah at the nurses' station made his lip curl. That do-gooder was the only person his mother had ever listened to, and he'd never understood why. What made *him* worth more than her own flesh and blood? It wasn't as if Golden Boy had amounted to anything—not when he spent his days catching drool off elderly chins and changing shitty sheets.

He managed to slip past unnoticed, but was spotted on his return.

"Taking a break?" Isaiah asked.

He jumped like he'd been caught stealing—which wasn't far off, given the good kick he'd given that machine before he finally coughed up the cash—and held up a pack of peanut butter crackers. The champagne idea had been a bust.

"Craving some nabs."

Isaiah nodded. "A woman came looking for you earlier. Did she catch you?"

He shook his head. And she never would, not if he had anything to do with it.

"Your momma's sure got some stamina," Isaiah went on. "We thought she was a goner a week ago."

Jimmy sighed. "That woman's tough as nails."

"How's she doing?"

"Still not moving. Can't be long now." It was impossible to keep the hope out of his voice.

"I'm sorry."

He waved away Isaiah's concern. "No matter. Her ranting and raving's worse."

"That's the dementia talking. Do you think her soul...?"

He caught the unspoken meaning. "Will go to heaven?" Bitterness seeped into his words. "I don't think she's got one."

Isaiah nodded again. "Want me to sit with you awhile? The last few hours can be the hardest."

He shrugged. "Sure."

Truth was, he'd never been much good with people. Not with Isaiah. Not with the women who'd tried to love him. Not even with the kids who shared his eyes. His mother had knocked the tenderness clean out of him early on, and the rest of the world had followed suit. But company in that room meant he wouldn't have to sit there alone with his mother's gaze drilling into him.

"I don't know how you do this," he said as Isaiah checked his mother's vitals.

"Do what?"

"Be with the dead every day."

Isaiah looked over at him. "Your momma's not dead—"

"Yet!"

"Shh! She might hear you." Isaiah gazed down at the shriveled shape in the bed. "It's an honor to be with the dying. To hold someone's hand through their darkest days, help ease their passing."

Jimmy marveled at this tolerance. He'd never been trained to simply stay put, steady and patient, without the need to turn everything into an opportunity. Some small, unnameable part of him wished he had.

"Do you believe in an afterlife?" he asked.

Isaiah let the question hang a moment. "My aunt went to her grave in her forties with a brain tumor, kicking and screaming. Far too young to die. She sure didn't believe at the end."

Jimmy grinned at his friend's loss of faith. Good to see that he'd finally wised up; learned there was nothing worth believing in except yourself. "How's *your* momma?"

Isaiah sighed. "Riddled with arthritis. I got a nice house here in Starkville, room all set up for her. But she won't leave that old shack, damn it, even though the damp in the walls is the last thing her joints need."

"Isaiah!"

"What?"

"I never heard you swear before."

A chuckle. "People change."

"I guess they do." Jimmy drummed his fingers on the bedside cabinet. Maybe he and Isaiah were more kindred spirits than he'd realized.

There was a stirring beneath the sheets. A murmur. Then a verbal tirade, as if the dying woman were speaking in tongues, only every word was clearly comprehensible.

"It never would've happened if my daddy had been around. He must've been turning in his grave, knowing his daughter was reduced to waiting on Black folks. But thanks to that gambling, drinking husband of mine, I had to go begging, didn't I? That no-account fool left me with nothing but debt. Even my kin turned on me. Only the preacher took pity. Poor foolish man. I always was good at cutting corners, learned that when I got married, had to. Pretty soon I squirreled enough away from the housekeeping to buy my first property. After that, I never looked back."

Jimmy wriggled in his seat. "Momma? You okay?"

Blank eyes turned to him. "Who are you?"

Her question stopped him cold. "Jimmy."

"Jimmy who?"

"Your son."

Her hands fumbled over the bedcovers. "Is this hell? Where's the blasted TV remote? I need to change the channel."

"You ain't in hell, Momma." He dropped his voice to a murmur. "But that's where you come from and that's where you're going mighty soon."

"Jimmy!"

He caught the shock on Isaiah's face and shrugged. "We both know it's true. She's not paying no mind to me, anyways."

She stared in Isaiah's direction. "Who's that?"

"You remember Mercy's son?"

"Why, surely I do. He told me I was going to heaven and it would be beau-tee-ful."

"He told you that?"

"At his daddy's funeral."

Isaiah's face went blank, and Jimmy let out a short, incredulous laugh.

"How old was he then? Five? You listened to a baby?"

She grunted. "Those words had the ring of truth. Always was a good boy, that one. Never lied. Unlike some I could mention."

He scowled at her, but she ignored him, her eyes wandering around the room.

"Why, I never!" she whispered.

Jimmy leaned in close. "What is it, Momma?"

"Your daddy's here."

"That's impossible."

"He's smiling at me."

Also impossible. The father he remembered was a violent drunk who'd met an early and well-deserved death at the end of a fist in a barroom brawl. A man who never had a kind word for his wife or son in his short, miserable life.

Her gaze shifted. "My momma's smiling too."

Yet another miserable SOB he'd been glad to see the back of. Did only the wretched show up at someone's deathbed? Then again, he couldn't think of any pleasant relatives.

"Oxygen deprivation makes people see things that aren't there," Isaiah whispered. "Humor her. It'll ease her passing."

"Where are they, Momma?" he asked.

"Right next to the bed. Your daddy has his hand on your shoulder."

A chill prickled down his left side, and he shuffled his chair closer to the wall. This was getting a little too spooky.

"They'd better treat me better in the hereafter," she rasped.

He patted her dry, wrinkled hand, and then, to his own surprise, left his hand sitting there. "I'm sure they will, Momma."

"Thanks for taking time off from your ministry to see me, son."

"What ministry?"

"At your church."

His eyes widened. "My church?"

"I'm so proud of you."

He glanced at Isaiah. "She's really lost the plot now."

"The dementia's making her hallucinations worse. Keep going along with her. You're doing great."

He smiled down at his mother. "I wouldn't have missed being here with you for anything." Hopefully, she heard the truth in his words. Not the reason. What he really wanted to experience was the exact moment he became a millionaire.

She stared straight at him. "Look after the cats, boy. I left them everything, but someone's gotta take care of my sweeties."

Was this dementia too? "You're dreaming, Momma."

Her eyes were clear now, startlingly so. "No, son. I've left them all my money. After they die, whatever's left goes to that animal-rescue society in town."

Jimmy opened and closed his hands. He should strangle the witch right here and now. Hasten her passing. But some survival instinct held him back.

"I'll take care of your cats," he promised. He'd look after them all right—introduce each and every one of those miserable creatures to the nearest lake.

"I love you," she said.

He blinked.

"I love you, son," she repeated.

His body froze up. Every wire in him blown.

A long, wet, crackling sound rattled out of her lips, and her chest collapsed as the air left her lungs. She seemed to cave in on herself. A childhood demon finally vanquished.

Isaiah took her pulse. "I'm so sorry. She's gone."

The room felt suddenly bare.

He shook his mother's shoulders. "Momma! Momma! Come back!"

But he could already feel the void inside her body.

Only a husk remained. And the questions—God, the questions—that raged through his mind.

Why had she told him she loved him? Was that her final twist of the knife, one last act of cruelty before she left him for good? She'd never even seemed to like him—always cussing him out, always swinging that big wooden spoon, always making him feel like a nuisance she'd been cursed with. How could she leave without explaining what she'd meant?

Yet beneath the anger coursing through his veins stirred something else, a sense of loss for the light she'd shone on him, dim and flickering though it had been. Those patched jeans, the soup ladled into a chipped bowl, the nights she'd sat awake beside his bed watching over his fever-racked body: they were more than duty. And in the space those memories opened up, a hollow he hadn't realized was there ached with sudden fullness. As miserable as his childhood had been, her small, grudging acts of care had meant something.

The words she'd spoken weren't a weapon.

They were the truth.

And now that they'd been said, he couldn't go back to the story he'd clung to. The certainty that he was unlovable, unworthy, and unwanted dissolved, leaving something raw and terrifying in its place. He wanted to shove it away, deny it, spit on it—but he couldn't.

Everything shifted.

Suddenly, the world seemed a little less hostile, a

little less cold. Maybe that was why, when one of the cats brushed against his leg, he didn't pull away. For the first time in his life, he let it stay.

CHAPTER EIGHT

The Furious Mother

Madeline seethed while her son slept. How could this be happening after everything she'd been through? Hadn't she suffered enough? Hadn't he?

If she'd believed in God, she would have shaken her fist at the ceiling. But she didn't have that consolation. Raised in a strictly atheist family, she had no deity to rail against, no prayer to cling to. Nor was there anyone to confide in, a supportive shoulder to lean into. Only the rhythmic sigh of machines kept her company in the airless hospital room. The blank white walls stared back at her, as indifferent as fate itself.

An elderly man ambled through the door. His aura of authority stamped his profession more clearly than any white coat.

"How's my favorite patient?" he asked.

"Asleep," she replied.

The doctor gave a small, wry smile. "Good! Your little man needs his rest. He's engaged in a mighty battle."

She pictured her son's blood cells at war with the enemy that hurtled through his veins, one that refused to be subdued by months of aggressive medication. Christian's symptoms had been mild at first: fatigue, pale skin, and bruises that bloomed on his body, which she'd put down to the same source as her own, hating herself for that. But after her husband's death, his illness erupted into bone pain and relentless vomiting. Something festered beneath the surface: a darkness deeper than what they'd already faced together. The devastating diagnosis—acute lymphocytic leukemia—had hurled her straight from one fire into another.

There'd been hope. Bucketloads of it. The survival rate for ALL was high, and she'd paid for the best care money could buy, admitting him to London's top children's hospital. Yet despite the best medical help in the country, her son's condition had continued to deteriorate as infection after infection ravaged his skeletal frame, his organs failing like lights switching off one by one.

"I thought your shift had finished," she said.

"It has," he admitted. "But I didn't want to leave you on your own. Not tonight."

Tears pricked her eyes. He knew, as she did, what little time remained. It was some small comfort to have company on this worst of journeys.

"How much longer will he be in pain?" she whispered, unsure which answer she feared most.

The doctor steepled his hands. "He's close now. I don't think he'll have to struggle much longer."

A ragged sigh escaped her lips.

He turned to her. "I wish you peace, Madeline."

"Are you talking about Christian? That he rests in peace? He's still here!" Her voice broke, rising higher than she intended.

He laid a warm hand on her shoulder. "I know. And I don't mean to sound callous. It's just...sometimes I think we say, 'rest in peace' to the wrong person. The dead don't struggle with loss. It's us—the living—who need solace."

A sob erupted from her mouth, quickly muffled by her hand as the bed covers rustled softly.

"Where there's life..." said the doctor.

"There's hope," she murmured. Not much, but as long as her son's heart kept beating, she'd fight for him.

Christian's eyelids fluttered open. "Mummmmmy?"

She grasped his hand. "I'm here, darling."

The doctor sat down next to his patient, who took up barely any space on the bed. "How are you, young man?"

Christian gave a thumbs-up.

"Sure?"

A slight nod, as if his head were too heavy to move.

"Good to hear!" The doctor patted the blankets and rose. "I'll give you two some time alone."

"Thank you," she murmured, eyes fixed on her son, drinking in every little detail of him while she still could. "What would you like to do, darling?" She didn't add, "in these last hours." What final wishes could she conjure, cooped up in a hospital room?

His gaze shifted to a dog-eared hardcover nearby.

"Shall I read to you?" she asked.

Another nod.

"Which part?"

"From the start," he croaked.

Her voice shook on the opening line. "All children, except one, grow up."

After a few chapters, he spoke up.

"*I'm* flying to Neverland, Mummy."

She caressed his face. "Are you, darling? When?"

"Soon."

The conviction in his tone sent a shiver through her. "I'm sure you'll enjoy it there. Can I come too?"

"No, silly."

Her hand drifted to the pearls at her neck. "Will you be happy?"

"Sooooo happy."

"Pinky promise?"

He lifted a tiny finger, and she hooked it with her own. "You know I love you to the moon."

"And back," he whispered, taking up their well-worn refrain.

"I love you as big as the universe."

"Mmmmmm." He let out a long sigh, eyes drifting shut again. Only the faint rise and fall of his chest told her they hadn't closed for the last time.

This had been the pattern for days: brief moments of lucidity, followed by ever-lengthening stretches of silence. During those quiet intervals, she clung to each flicker of movement, scanning for signs he still belonged to the land of the living. Not wanting to let him go. Not wanting to be abandoned, left with only grief for company. She stood alone on the edge of this precipice.

There was no comfort to be found in family. Her parents had made it clear early on they wouldn't watch their grandson's decline and remained holed up in their cottage, even at this late hour. Meanwhile, across the world in Singapore, her brother still hadn't responded to her SOS text. As for friends, she'd lost touch with them after her marriage. For a while, her husband's acquaintances had filled the gap, but those ties, too, had withered after his accident. She was even more isolated now than she'd been when she lost him a year ago.

She pulled at her pearls, an old reflex whenever she thought of Martin.

Her brother had brought him home to the Cotswolds a few years back, another commodities trader. As someone without any family of his own, he'd been grateful to them for welcoming him in: complimenting her mother's cooking, talking numbers for hours with the men, and inviting her on long walks in the countryside. He'd charmed them all. That was his strong suit.

She shook her head. Why was she wasting time thinking about her dead husband when her son was still here? Turning back to the blonde head on the pillow, she willed him to keep going. For her.

Time passed.

The doctor came and went, then came again.

"No change?"

"No change," she murmured.

He studied her face. "How are *you* holding up?"

"Fine." All that mattered was Christian.

"Have you eaten anything today?"

She rubbed her brow. "I'm not sure."

"Hmph! Guessed as much. I've arranged for you to be served dinner." He held up his hands to cut off her protest. "No, don't argue. I'll stay to make sure you eat it if necessary."

A reluctant smile tugged at her lips. "I promise I'll follow doctor's orders."

"Okay," he said as he gathered his notes. "You've got my number. If you need anything, even just someone to sit with you, call."

The roast beef and Yorkshire pudding revived her spirits. She saved the jelly and custard for Christian, just in case a miracle occurred and he felt hungry again. Where there was life...

She'd just pushed her empty dinner plate aside when he stirred again.

"Is it lunchtime?" he asked.

"Dinner. Want some jelly and custard?"

He shook his head, eyes scanning the room.

"Daddy's funny, Mummy."

Her hand flew to her pearls, then her shoulders softened. "He passed, remember? Daddy's not here."

"Yes, he is."

Her grip on the pearls tightened.

"Where, darling?"

Soft brown eyes turned upward. "In the air. Upside down, like a clown."

In life, Martin had been more magician than clown:

a master of misdirection. Still, she followed her son's gaze up to the ceiling tiles. Was Christian seeing shapes in the swirling dot pattern overhead?

A giggle bubbled out of him. "Daddy's juggling babies."

"Are they okay?" Her voice trembled.

"They're laughing. He's catching them in his palm and tickling them."

She gulped. They must be tiny.

"How many are there?"

"One, two, three," he said, as though counting them.

Her lips quivered. Before Christian, there'd been three pregnancies that hadn't come to term. Not surprising given the treatment her body had endured. Her son had never been told about those early losses. The thought that he could name what she'd mourned in silence made the room tilt, as if the border between life and death, memory and miracle, had suddenly dissolved. Could he see her lost little ones? Did they have souls? If that was the case, the afterlife had made a grave mistake entrusting them to Martin.

The afterlife! What was she thinking? She hadn't been raised to believe in that sort of guff. And after everything she'd endured, why would she? There'd been no God to rescue *her*. Logic insisted that her son's vision was the morphine talking. But it wouldn't hurt to indulge this fantasy for Christian's sake, just for a moment.

"Tell Daddy," she said through tight lips, "that he's not to go anywhere near those babies."

"He says he won't hurt them," said Christian.

"Your father's talking to you?"

Her son hesitated, as if listening. "Daddy's sorry."

"About what?"

"Everything."

She stared at him in bewilderment. It made no sense. She knew her dead husband had plenty to be sorry for, but how could Christian know that?

He'd been barely more than a toddler when the accident occurred—when Martin, chasing them in the car behind, lost sight of the road as he sped up to ram her slower Mini. Fixated on his fleeing family, he'd missed the bend ahead, drifting into the other lane when the asphalt curved. By some miracle, he'd managed to avoid hitting anyone else, slipping through a gap in traffic before embracing a tree. Nor had he managed to strike her car. To take her and Christian with him. If he had, then there truly would have been no justice in this world.

She swallowed hard. "Is he being punished?"

"Who?"

"Your father."

"No, silly. No one gets told off in Neverland. But he is very, very, very, to the moon and back, sorry. Says he'll make it up to you. He pinky-promised."

Her brow furrowed. Martin had always mocked the rituals she shared with their son. "Are you sure you're not making this up?"

"He loves us," Christian insisted.

She let out a short, disbelieving laugh.

"He does, Mummy. Really and truly, hope to die if I tell a lie." He raised a weak hand and traced a cross on his chest.

She gently lowered it. "Oh, darling, don't strain yourself. I believe you."

A faint smile curved his lips before his eyes drifted shut again.

She gazed at the ceiling as he slept. Was Martin's ghost really staring down at her? She certainly hoped not. She'd had enough of him in life and didn't want to experience him in death as well. And yet...there'd been a time when she couldn't get enough of him. Her family had felt the same, championing their match, delighted by how attentive he was. Wherever she went, he was there. Watching her. Wanting her. Making her feel seen. And she, as the least favored child, had found that impossible to resist.

She'd been on the verge of flying off to her dream job as a foreign correspondent when he persuaded her to stay, gifting her the string of pearls in lieu of the engagement ring they'd soon choose together. Even then, she'd remained footloose and fancy-free, enjoying the company of a wide circle of friends. It was only after the wedding that a steel net materialized around her. Bit by bit, the walls closed in. Shame kept her trapped.

The evening deepened. Hour after hour, the doctor came to check on Christian, keeping vigil alongside her as her son's life ebbed away. His skin slowly cooled beneath her fingertips. Death had its claws in him already.

She pressed a gentle kiss to his forehead. "I'll miss you so much."

A whisper. "I'm here, Mummy."

She glanced upward. "Is Daddy?"

"Uh-huh."

"What's he saying now?" she asked.

"Nothing."

"Nothing?"

"He's waiting."

She didn't need to ask for what.

Christian lapsed back into silence. It seemed as if each time he woke, there was a little less of him. She glared up at the ceiling. It wasn't right. It wasn't fair. At best, Martin had ignored Christian in life. How dare he get to be with their son after she lost him for good.

The truth about her husband had spilled out inside the funeral home when an elderly couple approached the front pew.

"Are you related to Martin?" the man asked.

Dry-eyed, she stared up at them. She'd barely spoken since he died, unable to convey the depth of her grief to anyone.

Her father pointed toward her. "This is his wife. Who are you?"

"His parents."

She gasped.

"Martin didn't have any parents," her father said flatly.

"Is that what he told you?" The woman held out a

black-and-white photo of a young boy. Unmistakably Martin.

Her father gestured stiffly to the far end of their pew. "There's room down there." After they sat, he leaned close to her ear. "What kind of people must they be for Martin to deny their existence?"

No one in her family spoke to them.

Apart from her.

At the reception, Martin's mother pulled her aside, scanning the exposed skin on her face, arms, and legs.

"You know, don't you?" Madeline said.

"I'm so sorry, my dear. If he hadn't cut us off, we'd have warned you. There were some...incidents, with a girl back home. After the police got involved, he vanished, and we never heard from him again."

The woman's grief mirrored her own. Not for Martin's death, but for his life. And in that moment, the floodgates inside her finally opened, and she burst into tears. Released at last from her cage of silence.

But freedom came without a map. She'd shaken off his shackles at last, only to find herself adrift. She had no idea how to move forward as a woman alone, having lost trace of her old friends and feeling betrayed by her family's ongoing loyalty to Martin. And before she could even begin to try, her son's illness consumed everything.

Toward midnight, the pauses between Christian's breaths grew longer.

His eyes suddenly flew open. "Muuuuummmmmy!"

"What is it, darling?"

"I have to go."

She threw herself over him.

"Don't leave me!"

His voice grew distant, thin as a thread. "I came 'cause of daddy."

Her breath caught. For a second, she wasn't in the hospital room anymore but back in the wreckage of her marriage: the slammed doors, the whispered apologies, the red marks hidden under sleeves. Could it be true? That this small, shining soul had chosen to step into that chaos for her? Disbelief warred with something softer, something dangerously like gratitude.

"What?" she choked.

"You needed me. Daddy was bad."

"How do you know?"

She'd done everything she could to protect her son from the truth. Bitten her tongue. Hidden her bruises. Had he heard his father's shouting through the walls? Her screams? What did he mean by *you needed me*: as if he'd been born to give her strength. It made no sense. But then, neither did Martin cradling her lost babies on the ceiling.

"You should leave too, Mummy."

"With you?" she whispered. Following her son into whatever waited beyond was tempting. What else did she have to live for? But the thought of crossing paths with Martin again was not so appealing.

"No! *Here*. Go everywhere, Mummy."

The string of pearls broke under the pressure of her hand.

That had been her dream as a child: to travel, to see the whole wide world. She'd driven her parents mad with her spontaneous escapes across the countryside. It was why she'd taken that job as a foreign correspondent in the first place.

How did Christian know? The thought pierced straight through her, sharper than grief. Her heart twisted. Every cell in her body screamed to follow him, to slip into the darkness where he was going and never come back. But he was asking her for something harder. To stay. To keep breathing in a world that would feel desolate without him, and somehow fill it with life again.

"I'll come with you," he whispered, closing his eyes again.

"You can't."

"Yes...I can."

The machine attached to his arm started shrieking, raising the alarm.

He was gone.

The silence that followed was deafening. Too vast. Too final. Her body folded around his, clinging to the weight of him as if she could keep his spirit there by sheer will. A sound escaped her throat, low and broken, the kind she hadn't made since the night Martin's violence first shattered her world.

And yet, even through the roar of her grief, his words still lingered. *Go everywhere, Mummy.* By some strange twist of fate, his final wish was her deepest desire. And she could take him with her on her adventures. His ashes would travel the globe.

How strange that everything—every terrible event—had led her back to where she'd been before accepting Martin's proposal at that airport. As if some guiding hand had shaped it all. She'd never believed in that sort of thing.

And yet...here she was.

CHAPTER NINE

The Abandoned Trailer Trash

A dull cramp bloomed in Ashley's belly, low and insistent, like a knot tightening deep inside her. Twenty minutes later, it returned—stronger this time, a violent spasm ripping through her core—and she braced herself against the kitchen counter, breath hitching.

When the spasm loosened, she forced herself to think. There was no rush to get to the hospital. According to pregnancy books at her local library, three bus rides away, childbirth was a long, drawn-out process. The plan was to leave only when contractions hit the five-minute mark. That way, her husband could stay at work for as long as possible.

So instead of texting him after the pain eased, she set the kettle to boil, poured a weak cup of coffee, and lowered herself onto the trailer's built-in seat with care—partly for the sheer bowling-ball weight pressing down on her pelvis, mostly because the stained, sagging cushions felt permanently fused with ground-in grime. Who knew what nefarious activities had taken place there?

A local rag had called her trailer park the "ghetto of

all ghettos", the last stop before homelessness. Since she and Noah had moved in, the van next door had been torched, and someone was stabbed behind the laundry block in broad daylight. However, it was the only place they could afford to rent in Las Vegas. A crib would be squeezed in somewhere after the baby outgrew the bottom drawer they'd set aside for the first month. Their trailer might not be much, but it was home—the first she'd ever really known.

Another contraction twisted through her. She checked the clock. They were down to ten minutes apart.

Already?

She peered through a dirt-speckled window. The lot looked deserted. There was no one around to assist should things go south. But she still hesitated to call her husband home from his shift. Every dollar counted. Nevada was one of the most expensive states to give birth. They'd both worked two jobs for years before daring to ditch birth control.

Her hand caressed the taut skin over her belly. "Stay in there a bit longer, little one."

She could only hope that this was an obedient child. That she'd do this right. That she'd finally be surrounded by the warm and loving family she'd always craved. She glanced at the only photo she had of her parents on a nearby shelf. The image of two people cradling a small bundle as they smiled at the camera had faded over time, as had her memories of them. They might as well be strangers.

Early on in life, there'd been a car accident on a rain-slicked road that had sent her parents' sedan over a cliff. Somehow, she'd been thrown free from her seat with the family dog in hot pursuit. Ace had wrapped himself around her like a shield, taking the brunt of the impact on his own body. She hadn't noticed the blood seeping through his fur as they waited together on an isolated road for help to arrive. He gave his life to save hers.

After that, she'd been shuffled between a series of increasingly disinterested relatives. A bed here, a couch there. Fed and clothed, little more. Meeting Noah had been her first piece of luck. They'd clicked in freshman year and obtained court approval to marry at seventeen so she could live with his family when her own ran out of patience.

Eventually, like so many before them, they drifted to the magnetic center of their state, chasing the mirage of Vegas prosperity. Not at the slots, but in uniforms and name tags. She worked reception and cleaned hotel rooms; he parked cars and hauled bags. Together, they made up part of the city's invisible army: unseen, unheard, but happy together.

A hot spike speared through her.

Soon followed by another.

Five minutes apart now.

Panic rose like bile. She fumbled for her phone and typed out a frantic message to Noah: *Come home. It's time*. She couldn't do this alone.

Pain didn't just rip anymore. It shredded every

fiber of her being. Again and again and again.

Two minutes apart.

This baby was coming, ready or not.

She slid onto the floor, seeking the stability of hard vinyl against her back. Yanking a dish towel from the oven handle, she jammed it under her hips. Her abdomen clenched—tighter, hotter—the edges of her vision pulsing white. Cramps merged, the next cresting before the last had drained away: like surfing several waves at once. The world narrowed to breath and burning.

And then the pain broke, and she was dumped on a distant shore, the world peeling away like old wallpaper. The hum of the interstate dissolved into stillness. The hardness against her back disappeared. The ache, the fire, the breathless clenching—gone. What filled her now wasn't relief but an impossible weightlessness, and the shock of no longer hurting. She found herself staring down at her body, watching it color the vinyl red. Then her vision stretched, moving beyond the sand-dusted window, the trailer park, and the sprawling, glittering metropolis of Las Vegas, until the city shrank to a single speck beneath her.

A dark, velvety space opened ahead with a pinprick of light glowing at its core. She moved toward it without hesitation, fear slipping from her like a discarded cloak. Two luminous forms hovered within the radiance. Though their features were blurred, their energy rang through her like music she'd always known. She flew into their embrace.

Her mother's voice vibrated inside her. "My love."

"You've been so brave," said her father, his warmth folding around her.

After what felt like an eternity held in their light, she pulled back.

"Am I dreaming?"

The words formed in her mind, yet somehow her parents heard them. A rush of pure, melodic energy—not laughter, but joy made audible—answered. *You've only just woken up.*

Understanding unfolded inside her: Earth had been the dream. The sea of living brilliance surrounding them, familiar and vibrant, was her real home.

"Is this heaven?"

"You could call it that," replied her mother. "Many do, but what you see is simply life in its purest form."

A question rose within, tentative and aching. "Should I be here? I stopped believing in God long ago." She didn't add that her faith had drained away in direct proportion to the level of care she'd received from her extended family over the years.

"God doesn't care whether you believe or not, my love," her mother communicated.

"Spirit is your natural state," added her father. "You never leave it."

A frown tugged at her, or it would have, if her new form allowed such things.

"That doesn't make any sense. I've been living my life on Earth."

A gentle pulse of light rolled off her father before he spoke. "A portion of your consciousness pretends it's living in physical reality. Most of you stays here."

Against all reason, everything he said made perfect sense. It explained why she'd slipped away from her body so easily. She focused on their glowing shapes, searching for signs of trauma.

"Did you suffer in the car accident?"

"Not at all," her mother pulsed.

"Our souls left our bodies before impact," said her father.

"Is that a thing when we die?" she asked him.

"Usually. Though some spirits choose to experience the death blow."

"Why on earth would anyone want to do that?"

Her parents' energy shifted with palpable amusement at her phrasing.

"It's part of the fun of creation," said her mother.

She thought of Ace, of her lonely years with indifferent relatives, the shame of the trailer park.

"How can suffering be fun?"

Her father's tone turned serious. "Earth is a purpose-made playground where spirits sample all sorts of experiences. The worst and the best."

"Like trying on new clothes?" A flash of the shapeless dresses she'd bought over the last few months came to mind. Putting on pregnancy weight was its own form of suffering.

More laughter shimmered around her.

"Yes," her father replied. "Source is expanding Its

understanding of Itself in all kinds of realms. Earth is the only place where we choose to forget who we are. That's what makes it so special. Our adventures there are intense, but we choose to have them."

"You chose to leave me?" But even as she said the words, they didn't ring true.

Her mother was gentle in reply. "You chose to experience life without parents, just as we chose to experience dying young. There was no abandonment, only contract."

Something inside her eased. An ache she hadn't known she carried uncoiled into light.

"Am I dead, then?"

Her father's energy twinkled. "You're...visiting."

A deep longing opened within her. She loved Noah and her baby fiercely, but she also knew how brief their time apart would seem here.

"Can't I stay?"

Her father reached for her, if a field of light could have a hand. "Dear one, before you were born, you chose to die and return to Earth—to take this encounter back with you."

"Why?"

"To help others understand," said her mother.

"Understand what?"

"That there's no need to kneel or beg. Source just wants a relationship with those on Earth. You can talk to It like a friend. Before you incarnated, you volunteered to spread this message, to remind people that they're loved, they're seen, and they're heard.

Source is ever watchful, and we are all part of It."

This was news. She had a mission on Earth. An important one. She, the girl from the "ghetto of all ghettos," was an ambassador. Go figure.

"Would you like a tour before you go?" her father asked.

Her mother beckoned. "Come!"

They drifted through a garden, greener and richer than any she'd seen before. Leaves shimmered when she passed, as if reacting to her presence. Exotic blooms pulsed with colors she couldn't name. From yards away, she could count the stamens on each flower, zoom in to the friendly face of a bee. *Was better eyesight a perk of being dead?*

"Earth seemed so real," she murmured, "but this... this feels realer."

Her parents laughed.

"That's because you get to experience the full power of who you are," said her father.

They glided past a radiant spirit holding a book, light flowing from its form like molten gold. Any flowers this stream touched blossomed brighter. Children darted through the rainbow of color, wild with joy. Watching them, she wished she could join in. Stay forever.

Suddenly, a smaller, vibrant spark zipped past those playful spirits and pulsed against her: a chaotic bounding energy of pure, unconditional love.

A jolt shot through her.

Ace.

The memory of his fading warmth on that isolated road dissolved away. He hadn't been lost. He'd simply come home first. And just like that, the last residue of her guilt and sorrow evaporated. The reunion with her family was now complete.

Ahead rose a vast towering structure, luminous and quietly imposing.

"This is the Hall of Healing," her mother said. "When people return in tragic circumstances, they're offered time for reflection, so the soul can process its death."

Light spilled from its walls in slow, rippling waves, brushing against her like warmth remembered as they drifted onward toward a shimmering boundary where the radiance intensified to blinding brilliance.

Her mother's presence spoke, "Now, child, feel The Whole."

An ocean of ecstatic love—nonjudgmental, ceaseless, infinite—engulfed her. She became every soul, every moment of creation, every instance of joy and sorrow, and understood the why of her mission with complete clarity: people needed to remember they were part of Source, what Earth called God. That Its power lived within them.

With that realization, the emotion swelling inside her grew too vast to contain. As she eased away from the field, it branded her with unshakable knowing of the truth she'd just felt. She would carry it with her forever.

They wandered on. Past a being in a white robe

communicating with an enthralled audience of thousands. Past an entire city made of light. Up into the stars. The entire cosmos unfolded before them. Time no longer existed. She lost herself in wonder.

At last, her father's glow dimmed. "It's time."

"For what?" she asked.

"For you to go back."

"Do I have to?"

"No," her mother replied gently. "But you want to go home."

"*This* feels like home."

"Someone needs you."

As if on cue, a faint cry echoed through the light.

She started. "Is that my baby?"

Her father nodded. "She's awake."

"She?"

"You've given birth to a beautiful baby girl," said her mother.

A gentle tug pulled at her, then a steady, irresistible force.

"I don't want to lose you again," she called into the void, as she was dragged farther and farther away.

The cry came once more—louder this time, insistent, alive—and a sharper pull seized her.

Her father's voice was fading. "You never lost us."

The twin spheres of white light dimmed, like stars disappearing into the dawn of a new day, and the connection snapped.

She dropped into darkness.

Sensation returned. The wet floor of the trailer,

warm with her own blood, pressed against her spine as her mother's voice echoed through her mind: *We love you.*

Then another voice. Closer. Harsh with fear. "Ashley Bella!"

Her eyelids peeled open. Noah stood in the doorway, his face white as a ghost. A gurgle rose up inside her and she let out a short, hysterical laugh. If anyone was a ghost around here, it was her.

Then a sound stopped her—a soft mewl, like a kitten.

Her heart clenched.

Any lingering desire to return to her parents evaporated.

Someone needed her.

Someone she needed just as much.

CHAPTER TEN

The Lost Boy

Mercy drew a ragged breath. Seconds passed. Minutes. Isaiah leaned forward in his chair, fingers poised to check her pulse. Then another small, wet inhalation slipped through her cracked lips.

He sighed with relief and slumped back in the chair he'd pulled close to the rickety bed frame. It was the same iron torturing device she'd shared with his daddy. His momma had refused to give it up when his father passed. She refused again when he sent a brand-new bed to her shack with his first nursing paycheck: that one sat unused in the front room "for company." And she'd refused to give it up even as her life tapered toward its end.

"I ain't moving," she'd replied when he insisted she return to hospital for good.

Nor had she taken up his suggestion to move into the assisted care place where he worked, so he'd be on hand. Even when he begged her to sign on the dotted line for a rare available room, she was unyielding. "This is where your daddy lay, and this is where I'm staying till the Lord calls me home."

He didn't remember his father's body lying in state on the bed, didn't recall his death or the funeral where apparently he'd caused quite the scene. What he recalled was the silver toy plane he'd received as a gift—how flying it upward made him feel connected to an intangible cloak of love, as if the skies themselves protected him. His momma used to say that was his daddy watching over him like an angel, and he'd believed her. He shook his head at his youthful stupidity.

Another long pause between her breaths.

Not long to go now. Her best Sunday dress was already laid out at the foot of the bed for her final showing.

He'd sorted through her few possessions during the long hours of his vigil. Up on a high shelf he'd found his old toy plane, not dusty like other knick-knacks but gleaming silver, as if his momma polished it up on the regular. How strange. He rolled it between his fingers, wondering why she'd bothered.

This toy was the closest he'd ever come to flying. There'd been no need for him to catch a real-life jet with his entire life spent within the confines of his home state. The farthest he'd ever gone was Jackson for nursing school, and that time away from his beloved momma had felt like exile. He'd stayed in Starkville ever since.

He glanced around the familiar bedroom where he'd slept on a cot beside her until his marriage. His wife had refused to move into the shack after their honeymoon. Fair enough. Connie Moore hadn't spent one dime on the property during her decades of ownership. It was only after her passing that conditions improved. Holes were patched, the walls repainted, and the rusty old roof, which used to provide a free indoor shower every time it rained, was finally exchanged for solid steel. How good of the animal-rescue folks to take time out from saving orphaned cats and dogs to fix up his momma's home.

A soft murmuring seeped through the thin chipboard wall separating the two rooms in the house. His wife and children had retreated to the kitchen to allow him to sit alone with her as the end drew near.

"O Lord God, we give you thanks for all the mercies, which during her life you bestowed on our beloved," said his wife.

"Amen," replied a squeaky voice.

"Double amen!" added a squeakier one.

He didn't join in this prayer. His footsteps hadn't crossed a church threshold in years. By choice. Somewhere along the line, his belief had thinned, like air at high altitude.

Maybe the rot set in when he'd looked at Jimmy's face after the pastor had that weird spell. He hadn't wanted to work at the drugstore that day. The thermometer hit a hundred degrees early on, and bathing naked in the wash tub under a magnolia tree beat sweating on his bike. But his momma had insisted.

"You ain't got nothing better to do."

She hadn't added that they needed the money, that every scrap helped pay for his ongoing education, now that it had been decided he'd be the first in their family to attend college. This was a matter about which he had no choice. It was "what your daddy would have wanted." And there was no arguing with a dead man, especially one sainted by his widow.

Jimmy had been the other delivery boy employed that summer. He was dragged in each morning by his mother, loudly proclaiming her determination to ensure "he didn't turn into a layabout like his father." Two years older, he seemed like a man to Isaiah—someone to look up to for lack of a better option. But Jimmy barely noticed him, except to toss a "You got this, kid!" whenever a new order came through. Most of the time Isaiah was the one pedaling out on the dusty road, while Jimmy stayed in the cool, ogling girls in short dresses getting ice-creams across the street. However, he'd tagged along when he heard the pastor was poorly.

The house next to the church was deathly quiet when they rode up.

"You think he's in there?" Isaiah asked.

"Oh, he's in there all right—probably cooking up another sermon to scare the fun outta folks."

Isaiah pondered this new spin on the sacred words he heard each week in church as Jimmy pushed open the front door.

"Shouldn't we knock first?"

"I live here, remember." Jimmy stepped inside. "Pastor Thomas? You here?"

There was no response.

"You think we should check the rooms?"

Jimmy stepped back and held out an arm. "After you!"

Isaiah entered the house, his heart thudding, the air inside thick and still.

They found the pastor on the living room floor, collapsed in a pool of vomit. Jimmy took one look and bolted—muttering something about getting his momma—leaving Isaiah alone with a body that looked more dead than alive.

Everything after that was a blur. There was shaking—first of his own knees, then of the pastor as he tried to wake him. Next came praying: *Release me, Lord Jesus Christ, from my suffering. I mean, Pastor Thomas. Release him from his suffering. But don't let him die! They'll blame me for not looking after him proper.*

Then came the shouting when Jimmy returned with his mother. And the look on Jimmy's face as he wound a finger next to his ear and pointed at the pastor. Isaiah could see clear as daylight that Jimmy thought his benefactor was cuckoo-crazy. And he would know. He lived with the man. Maybe Pastor Thomas wasn't right in the head. *Had he been a fool to heed the pastor's words of a Sunday, as his momma instructed?*

Isaiah sighed now at the naïve boy he'd been. Fancy paying attention to that loser. Jimmy had never amounted to much. Even years later, when his own momma lay dying, he'd radiated self-interest. Isaiah had known his company wasn't wanted at her deathbed—Jimmy just didn't want to be alone—but he'd joined them anyway. He took the Nightingale Pledge seriously. His life was devoted to service and to the high ideals of the nursing profession, even if it meant supporting a scumbag like Jimmy.

It was after Connie Moore's passing that his faith finally faltered. Two momentous events occurred in its wake that sealed his disillusionment with religion.

First, Jimmy found Jesus. Truly found him. Said he'd been born again and started spreading God's word with a fire that lit up the entire congregation. He filled every conversation with scripture and salvation, his face lit from within like a man fresh from the river.

Second, he announced his momma had been admitted into heaven.

"They let *everyone* in," he'd said, grinning with his new unshakable joy.

That had been the last straw for Isaiah. If they could let that mean old bag through those pearly gates, the one who'd made his momma's life such misery, then heaven was no place for him. Something inside him closed after that, quiet and final, and he stopped attending church for good.

A small movement snapped him out of his thoughts. His momma had shifted her head to look at him, her eyes wide and alert for the first time in a week, her face serene. He tugged at his collar as if he were caught in something private. *Wasn't it meant to be her reviewing the past, not him?* However she seemed at peace with her life, even her death.

A leathery palm covered his hand on the blanket.

"How's my boy?"

He leaned closer. "How are *you*?"

"I'm good, son. Ready and willing to meet my maker when He calls me. I can hear His footsteps approaching."

"Momma—"

She patted his hand. "Aw, don't grieve for me, baby. I'm off to see your daddy and that brings a smile to my heart."

"You really believe there's something after this?"

"I surely do, and so do you," she replied with a faint smile. "When you were little, you told me that when we wake in heaven, we're happy."

He frowned. Jimmy's momma had said something similar, but he hadn't believed her. *Was it true?*

"I don't remember saying that."

"You don't remember us sparkling, and your daddy watching over us?"

He leaned back in his chair and crossed his arms. "Sounds like I had a real imagination."

"You shone a light into people's souls that day—ain't no one who was there could forget it." Her eyes lit up as she spoke, a shimmer of the younger mother who'd once held his world together.

It hit him hard then, what he was about to lose, and he swallowed against the sudden tightness in his throat.

Still, he scoffed. "How can you believe in God after everything He's put you through? Living in this broken-down shack your entire life, working for those folks who never once said thank you?"

"He answered my prayers, didn't He?"

"But you've been sick, and you've been poor your whole life." His hands sliced through the air, trying to capture the enormity of her suffering.

She met his gaze, steady and clear. "I didn't pray for me, baby, I asked for you. And God answered. When we had no money for your school things, Pastor Thomas organised special collections to help you through. When we couldn't pay rent, Miss Connie let me settle up in kind. Every time we were brought low, grace found a way."

This was too much. She'd gone too far.

He articulated his next words carefully. "Connie Moore didn't have a speck of decency in her entire soul."

His momma smiled gently. "She put on a sourpuss face, that's all. Said it stopped men from taking advantage. After your daddy passed, she never asked for rent till I had money again, just let me pay in tomato aspic. It was her who got me that job at her brother's drugstore so I didn't have to work on my knees no more. When we needed more money for your college tuition, she made him hire you, even with Jimmy already running errands. You remember delivering them medicines?"

He nodded, speechless.

His mother's hand tightened over his. "And God kept on giving, baby. When you needed letters to go to nursing school, our doctor gave you the highest recommendation. When you needed a place to stay in Jackson, the pastor found you a room with good people, folks who'd see you got fed and minded your books. See, child—see how blessed we've been!"

Tears rolled down his face. "Why, Momma, I never thought to count my blessings. I was too busy worrying over you. And to think all this time you were happy."

She reached up and brushed the wetness from his cheeks. "What more could I ask for? I had you. And when you were just a young'un, you told me heaven was real—right when I needed to hear it. I'm giving that back to you now, son. You should join Jimmy's church. The man's got a real knack with his flock."

He stiffened. "Jimmy's church? What, he buy it or something?" That would be right. Another madcap scheme to make his fortune after his mother cut him out of her will.

"He took over from Pastor Thomas when he retired," she replied, her voice trailing off.

"I can't believe the old pastor allowed that," he spat.

She breathed in and out a few times as if gathering her strength for a sprint. "He was the one who insisted Jimmy was the best candidate for the job."

"Pastor Thomas?"

"We all agreed. Jimmy's been visiting to pray over me. Brought one of his cats to keep me company. See, by the windowsill? Jimmy's got a peace about him these days that only the Lord can give. Just like

Pastor Thomas after that sick spell he had years ago. Remember?"

"Well, I never."

"Be happy, son." Her eyes bore into his, and a sudden clarity shot through him.

"I will, Momma. I promise!"

She closed her eyes and whispered, "That's my baby."

Her shoulders tightened, then fell still. And the last of her breath slipped away.

He leaned over the bed to shake her gently. "Momma?...Momma?"

The silence stretched. Then words rose in the next room, clear and strong.

The night has passed, and the day lies open before us. Let us pray with one heart and mind.

He fell to his knees beside the bed, weeping, his tears soaking into the worn floorboards. For a long while, he stayed there, head bowed, lips moving in whispered prayer. Morning crept through the thin curtains, touching her resting hands, his face, the faded quilt she'd mended a dozen times.

And in that hush, his spirit turned back into the arms of the Lord, just as hers had.

EPILOGUE

The Neverending Story

A blues band heralded Mercy's arrival into heaven. Her husband, who had never been one for displays of affection, pulled her close. Then her father took her hand and led her in a dance with her long-departed sister. Ancestors crowded around them, stretching back through generations to the very start of her lineage. She rested her weary soul in their waiting arms.

Because when we wake in heaven, our earthly struggles simply fall away.

Other souls made their entrance.

To the utter horror of Ethan's uptown parents—who'd spent years bragging about their son-the-future-surgeon—he became a specialist in near-death experiences. His partner supported him in this new calling, never questioning the sacrifices it demanded of them. Not even when they were forced to trade their beloved New York for small towns built around obscure universities in states where their relationship was, at best, politely ignored.

His field eventually gained enough respect for him to secure a position at a major university in California, where at last they were both embraced by a community that accepted them for who they were. By then, the rupture with his family was all but complete. Yet when he reached the other side, he was greeted without a moment's hesitation by his long-departed parents.

Because when we wake in heaven, there is only the memory of our love for one another.

The lives of the hippies were never the same after Doh's close brush with death. Shocked by his cousin's near loss, Shin felt inspired to become a Buddhist monk, a choice that brought him the contentment he'd once sought at the end of a pipe. Doh quit the takeout business and got a job as a custodian collecting trash at Disneyland, eventually working his way up to play Goofy. He shared a tiny apartment nearby with other cast members, his life Disneyfied, 24/7.

The other two were similarly shaken. Andres, freaked out, swore off drugs on the spot. For Eduardo, however, it took longer to find peace.

Dragged into dealing by a demanding uncle when he was still in grade school, he'd used drugs to survive and remained in the trade simply because it was all he knew. A few years on, while running a job at Disneyland, he crossed paths with Doh again and stayed to watch Goofy prance down Main Street, joy in every step, ears flapping, ridiculous and free.

That was the final nail in the coffin of his old life.

He gave away his ill-gotten gains to the homeless and moved interstate so his past couldn't find him, taking a job as a janitor at a rough high school in the Midwest. There he lectured kids on the dangers of drugs. Eyes rolled. But one or two listened, and that was enough. When he finally crossed over, the first thing he saw was his beloved California shore, the kids he'd saved from tragedy waiting for him at the water's edge and the waves rolling in soft as breath.

Because when we wake in heaven, we see the afterlife as we pictured it, so that our passing may be eased.

Pastor Thomas went to sleep one night and woke up in a peaceful sanctuary, a dark-skinned man in a white robe smiling down at him. In that moment, he felt himself folded back into the oneness of God.

Because when we wake in heaven, it's as if we've stepped sideways into a parallel reality.

Aisha slipped in and out of heaven when a rip dragged her under the Gold Coast surf. One moment: light. The next: water, pressure, darkness. Then she burst back into the world coughing salt and sand, lungs burning, cheek pressed to the gritty shore. It was only when she staggered upright—alive, impossibly alive—that the deeper wave hit. Compassion crashed over her, fierce and shocking, washing away the last shadow of the past. Her anger at her family dissolved, as if it were the downy head of a dandelion blown away on the breeze.

Decades later, when her brothers could no longer pose a danger, she searched for them. Only Kaseem remained alive, confined to a run-down nursing home with motor neuron disease. If he'd had other family, they were no longer involved in his care, a nurse explained, clearly delighted by her visit. Through slurred speech, Kaseem conveyed his gratitude for her presence. Over many meetings, she received his love and deep regret for their estrangement. When his final breath came, she was there to guide him home.

Because when we wake in heaven, we may be given the chance to return—without knowing we've died—so we can change the course of the life we've been living.

Ọdẹwálé lived to a ripe old age, becoming a hunter and leader of his tribe. Upon entering heaven, he rushed to his father to ask for forgiveness. But it had already been given. His father's arms opened wide, and in that instant, all the years of guilt and silence lifted away, coolness settling over his spirit like shade after burning sun. Relief flooded through him.

Then came the remembering.

During his life review, he felt every wound he'd ever carved into his father's heart, welcoming the pain. Because when we wake in heaven, we can choose to experience the hurt we've inflicted on others to ensure we never commit such harm again.

Jimmy remained in the church until death. The role of pastor turned out to be the perfect fit for his jack-of-all-trades skills. He procured household goods from legitimate sources instead of shady ones, sweet-talked respectable insurance companies into providing coverage for his flock at fair rates, and even leaned on the local mafia to offer free fuel to struggling families. He'd kept his mouth shut after that gas-station incident. They owed him.

Most of his modest pay went to support the mothers of his children after he finally accepted his role as a father, where it was still wanted. He also reached out to the animal-rescue society, offering to fix up his mother's rental properties, starting with Mercy's.

As far as he was concerned, these were the best years of his life.

At heaven's gate, he was cheered in by an enormous crowd of souls he'd supported on Earth, plus a few ne'er-do-wells he'd traveled alongside before seeing the light. His mother beamed with pride on the sidelines.

Because when we wake in heaven, we are embraced by all those whose lives we've touched, in ways both good and bad.

At the end of her days, Madeline was escorted through the tunnel by her son, the two of them laughing and singing together.

"I can fly! I can fly! I can fly!"

Her first husband waited on the other side, and she greeted him warmly. She'd long since forgiven his cruelty, not wanting to be stuck in some kind of karmic hell with him forever. Eventually, forgiveness came from love alone. He'd blessed her with Christian, her only child, whose presence she felt every step of her journey to becoming an in-demand travel blogger.

In Bali, she met a kind man and settled down with him, welcomed by his family despite her refusal to join in their ancient rituals. There was no need for her to seek consolation in religion. She knew her son was waiting beyond the veil.

When her time came to leave Earth, she dove straight into the light. Only then did she understand that every act of love, every forgiveness, had been a rehearsal for the afterlife, allowing her to meet Martin without the old wounds between them.

Because when we wake in heaven, we dissolve into the whole. There is no you and me, only we. Different melodies of the same eternal song.

Ashley had to swallow down jealousy when her husband returned to spirit before she did.

"Why him and not me?" she wondered aloud to her empty house after the wake.

A gust of wind rushed through an open window, rattling the frame containing her parents' photo. It lurched forward just enough to knock a larger picture to the floor. She picked it up. Her first grandchild smiled out at her through unbroken glass and she nodded, understanding at last. Her grandbaby needed her.

It didn't ease the ache, though. To soothe her soul, she learned how to meditate, touching heaven in brief periods of illumination. In those still hours she began to sense a greater pattern, threads of love stretching between worlds, holding everything together.

She often felt her husband's presence beside her as she rocked their descendants on the front porch of the house where they'd raised their own little ones. She'd bought it with a sudden windfall soon after her near-death experience. A newly discovered financial inheritance came to light, shares acquired before the accident, the paperwork somehow lost in the mail. Turned out her parents *were* true to their word. They'd never abandoned her. Knowing this changed everything.

And when death finally called, she answered without fear, because she'd long known that when we wake in heaven, it feels like coming home.

Isaiah was greeted in heaven by a full host of souls celebrating his triumph. He'd achieved his mission to share the truth of the afterlife. And people had listened.

"Well done, son," said Mercy, welcoming him back.

"You were right, Momma," he said, falling into her arms. "About Jimmy, God, heaven, everything."

He'd become the most devoted member of Jimmy's church after his mother's passing, carrying forward the message she'd shared with him on her deathbed, one he'd unknowingly given her as a child. And now he understood: the circle was complete. None of us hold heaven alone. We hold it for one another.

Because even before we wake in heaven, we can find it within us, awakening in the heart the moment we remember who we are.

Heaven's door kept revolving as the Source extended into every domain, seeking to know Itself in as many ways as It could. Some oversouls had fingers in the past, others in the future, and a few had their hands buried deep in a smorgasbord of timelines.

Possibilities beckoned. They could venture to other planets. Dive into alternative dimensions. All at once. Altogether.

Only on Earth did souls forget their origin.

But a few remembered.

They came as messengers to weave the Word of Source into stories told by firelight, etched onto pages, or shared across social media, whatever form would work to open the listener's heart. The same truth was carried from one end of the world to the other: of the worthiness of each of us, of compassion for our suffering, and of the unconditional love that vibrates through the universe.

Just there.

Within reach.

Waiting for you.

Glossary

The Grieving Widow

COPD	Chronic Obstructive Pulmonary Disease

The Estranged Daughter

Nene	Grandmother
Tasbih beads	Islamic prayer beads
Wog	Derogatory term for new Australian resident.

The Resentful Son

Ah-ah	Exclamation of surprise
Am	It
Àmín	Amen
Baba	Father; also used respectfully for an old man
Don	Have already
Ehen	Exactly
Ewé akoko	A sacred medicinal herb used in Yoruba burial rites

Fit	Can
Igbó	Marijuana
Ìgbò	One of the major ethnic groups of Nigeria
Ìrókò	Massive hardwood tree considered sacred
Ke	You must be joking
Má bìnú	Forgive me
Mama	Mother
My guy	Nigerian Pidgin term of camaraderie, similar to 'my friend' or 'bro'
Naira	Nigeria's national currency
O	Nigerian expression, indicating insistence
Òbàtálá	One of the major deities in Yoruba cosmology, associated with creation
Ọdẹ	Hunter
Ògún	A warrior spirit
Olùfẹ́ mi	My beloved
Ọmọ mi	My son
Sef	Nigerian Pidgin intensifier meaning 'even', 'indeed', or 'honestly'

Yahoo boy	Nigerian slang for a young man engaged in online scams, often involving romantic deception of foreign women.

The Optimistic Good-For-Nothing

RC	RC Cola

Acknowledgements

Thank you to the people of Mississippi who welcomed me with such warmth.

Thank you to Kate and Derek of the Oktibbeha County Heritage Museum, who shared their knowledge about the Black American community in Starkville. An extra-special shout-out to Kate, who served as my sensitivity reader for those sections of my story.

Thank you to my Yoruba sensitivity readers, Happiness and Mrs. Olaboade.

Thank you to the Australian Writers' Centre for pulling me out of my garret by accepting me into the *Write Your Novel* course, and to my beautiful friend Janice for suggesting it in the first place.

Thank you to the wonderful Words At Dawn, PWC, and Bad Mother crews for keeping me inspired to write, as well as for your delightful company.

Thank you to my readers: Christine, Helene, Kate and the many members of my writing groups who offered to provide overall feedback on my story.

Thank you to my super-encouraging editor, Maria, for providing suggestions that fit so well with this book's intention.

Thank you to Julie Postance at Iinspire Media for her brilliant publishing guidance.

And thank you to my family and friends who helped keep the flame of my writing dream alive, even when my candle burned low.

Information about life in Starkville was obtained from these sources:

Jerry Jones, *The Book of Needmore: ws One, Two and Three.*

Sadye H. Weir & John F. Marszalek, *Black Businessman in White Mississippi 1886-1974*, University Press of Mississippi, 1977.

Douglas L. Conner & John F. Marszalek, *A Black Physician's Story: Bringing Hope in Mississippi*, University Press of Mississippi, 1985.

About The Author

Tan Lee is a high-school science teacher in Melbourne, Australia. The proud parent of two beautiful daughters who have flown the nest. An avid outdoor adventurer who finds a home in the bush. A fresh-food fanatic. Gardener on training wheels. Star gazer. Someone who takes time out of their day to watch sunrises and sunsets. Who gets lost down archaeology and spirituality wormholes on TikTok. And a long-time fledgling novelist.

Contact Tan Lee

www.writertanlee.com

Instagram: writertanlee
Tiktok: writertanlee
Facebook: Writer Tan Lee
Substack: Writer Tan Lee

JOIN TAN'S ONLINE REFLECTION GROUP

You can sign up here:

https://writertanlee.com/contact/

SUBSCRIBE TO TAN'S NEWSLETTER

https://substack.com/@writertanlee3

www.ingramcontent.com/pod-product-compliance
Lightning Source LLC
LaVergne TN
LVHW090956080826
845145LV00003B/1021

* 9 7 8 1 7 6 4 3 9 3 1 4 0 *